A Cold, Hard Case

A Cold, Hard Case

A Luca Mystery

Book 5

by Dan Petrosini

Copyright © Dan Petrosini 2018

All rights reserved. No part of this publication may be reproduced, stored in a retrieval system, or transmitted, in any form or by any means, electronic, mechanical, photocopying, recording or otherwise, without the prior written permission of the publishers.

The novel is entirely a work of fiction Any resemblance to actual persons, living or dead, is entirely coincidental. For requests, information, and more, contact Dan Petrosini at dan@danpetrosini.com

Available in ebook and print.

Acknowledgments

Writing would not be possible without the love and support of my wife, Julie, and daughters Stephanie and Jennifer.

A special shout out to Squad Sergeant, Craig Perrelli, for his counsel, making sure I keep stories aligned with the real world of law enforcement

Other Books by Dan Petrosini

Third Chances – A Luca Mystery Book 4

The Serenity Murder – A Luca Mystery Book 3

Vanished – A Luca Mystery Book 2

Am I the Killer? – A Luca Mystery Book 1

The Final Enemy

Complicit Witness

Push Back

Ambition Cliff

Coming Soon – Book 6 - A Luca Mystery

Chapter 1

It was a strange conversation. The caller claimed to have information to solve a twenty-five-year-old murder. The woman identified the victim as seventeen-year-old Debbie Boyle. Pressing her for more, she became cagey, saying it was some sort of deathbed confession that she wanted to discuss in person. I jotted down her address and hung up.

I'd been in Naples, Florida, for several years, and the name Debbie Boyle didn't mean anything to me. Much as I wanted to do something other than chase petty thieves, I needed to check the cold case archives before heading into the sunshine.

Protocol was to pass the information to the detectives who'd worked the case. Plugging Debbie Boyle into the database, I was betting they were long gone.

A grainy picture of a pretty seventeen-year-old filled the screen. Shoulder-length, dirty-blond hair framed a petite nose and thick, dark eyebrows. Was her hair dyed? The kid was five foot three, a hundred and five pounds. It looked like she was wearing a school sports shirt.

Below the image was a summary:

Case Number 038231 - Detective Ernest Foster

Deborah Boyle, DOB 4/19/1976. Body found at Delnor-Wiggins Pass Park on the morning of May 15, 1993. Multiple stab wounds from a knife-like instrument. Blunt-force trauma at the back of the head.

No weapons found at the scene. Victim's brother, 7 years old, Brian Boyle was with her but did not witness attack.

Persons of interest -

John Wheeler - Boyfriend - With victim night of the homicide. Claimed he was also attacked, receiving a blow to his forehead causing him to lose consciousness. Unable to recall events of that night.

Clem Walker - Surf fishing near Wiggins Pass the night of the murder.

Spiro Papadakis and Diane Nielsen - Separately out beach walking in the area that night.

Matt Boralis - A 37-year-old Lee County man questioned for luring young girls at the park.

Lew Mackay - Placed at the park by witnesses but denied being there.

Evidence, case documents and interview notes filed in Records, Section 3, Row L, on November 15, 1996.

Weird, the report was filed exactly twenty-two years ago today. I leaned back. Detective Foster had put the case on ice in less than four years. Why? He seemed to have a parade of suspects. In my book, you don't call someone a person of interest if they've been cleared. Maybe it had to do with the way they uploaded cold cases when everything went online.

I punched an extension into the phone.

"Timmy, it's Luca. Can you dig out 038231 for me? . . . Nah, just the case file . . . Great, I'll be down in ten."

Chapter 2

A thin layer of dust darkened the top of the cardboard bankers box. I lifted the cover carefully. Greeted by a musty odor, I set the cover on the floor.

It was twenty-five years ago; didn't they use more paper back then? There were only four folders making up the case file, and they were thin. Did Timmy miss a box? I checked the tab on the lead folder: Deborah Boyle 4/19/76.

Black marker was used to write the case number and to strike through a red stamp that read *active*. The preprinted folder had no box for homicides, which are rare in Collier County. Someone checked the box marked *other*, penning *homicide* next to it.

No one had signed out the file since it went cold. That was strange. Nothing had come up in twenty-five years?

Stifling a sneeze, I flipped the lead file open. A head shot of Debbie Boyle was stapled to the left. It was the same one that was online but miles clearer.

Staring at the teenager, a tiny vibration ran across the base of my skull. That sensation hadn't occurred since my first homicide, the Barrow case. Ignorant at the time, I allowed myself to be bullied into arresting someone I didn't think did it.

Swallowing my pride was nothing compared to the guilt I felt when Barrow hung himself his first night in a cell. I knew I would continue to regret ignoring that biological alarm the rest of my life.

I wasn't going to make that mistake again.

* * *

"Hi, Frank. What are you reading?"

"Hey, Vargas. Got a strange call on a case, a kid, Debbie Boyle, was killed at Wiggins Park."

"A murder at Wiggins?"

"Twenty-five years ago."

"Oh, you scared me."

"It was a long time ago, and I don't wanna take shots at this Foster guy who led the investigation, but he did a piss-poor job on this one."

"What was the call about?"

I fished for the notepad. "A woman, Betty Kennedy, called in saying she had information that would solve the kid's murder."

"Who was the lead?"

"Detective Ernest Foster."

"Must be retired."

"Probably. Anyway, this Kennedy woman called in—"

"Was she in the case file?"

"No, but I didn't get through it all."

"Fill me in and we'll go see her."

"Boyle was at Wiggins with her brother; he was just seven, and a boyfriend, a twenty-two-year-old."

"How old was Boyle?"

"Seventeen."

"And she was dating a twenty-two-year-old?"

"I know, the kid lost her father when she was three. Probably looking for a father figure."

"A twenty-two-year-old father figure?"

"You know what I mean."

"Go ahead."

"They're at the beach late, and sometime around eight the girl goes missing."

"They kept a seven-year-old at the beach that late?"

"It's a question we need to check into. So, Boyle disappears. The boyfriend said she'd gone to the bathroom, and when she was gone too long he went to see what was going on."

"He left the kid alone?"

I nodded. "The boyfriend said he was attacked by someone and hit on the head. Claims he was unconscious and doesn't recall anything."

"How long was he out?"

"He said less than an hour. Said when he came to he went looking for his girlfriend and her brother. The brother was by the water's edge talking to a guy named Clem Walker, who was fishing. This Walker character has a shady past, a couple of arrests."

"What happened? Did they find the girl?"

"No, said they combed the area but couldn't find her."

"You think this boyfriend knew where she was?"

"He'd be the first on my list. Anyway, a guy camping finds her body early the next morning. She'd been stabbed repeatedly and died sometime between 10 p.m. and midnight."

"What happened to the boyfriend? He said he was attacked."

"Had a forehead wound from a blunt instrument, but it didn't appear too serious."

"You think it was self-inflicted?"

"Pretty convenient, don't you think? Feels damn suspicious."

"I know. He's out long enough to say he doesn't know what happened?"

"I didn't get to it yet, but his medical records better support a blow hard enough to knock his ass out."

"What did her brother say happened?"

I shook my head. "I scanned one interview, and Foster seemed to be leading the kid. It's another thing we need to look over when we open it."

"You're going to reopen the case based upon a quick read through?"

"And the call. Besides, why not? We got nothing but that handbag ring we're chasing."

"You got a feeling on this, don't you?"

She knew me better than I knew myself. "There's something here, Vargas."

"All right, let's go see Kennedy."

"Right after I check the box of physical evidence."

The catalog of objects collected from the crime scene was disappointing. What was I expecting? The items from the scene read like a picnic check list: a red cooler containing potato chips and Coke, a blanket, the victim's pocketbook, hair belonging to the victim, to her brother, and to John Wheeler, the boyfriend. There was a deck of cards, a magazine, a sand shovel, and a blue bucket.

Articles obtained from the autopsy were standard: bloodstained clothes, the victim's jewelry, fourteen dollars in cash, and her driver's license.

I pawed my way through the plastic-bagged items. Mold was visible and extensive. I wondered when the switch to paper bags had taken place and put the lid back on the box.

Chapter 3

There were six officers involved in a stakeout we'd set up at the Saks in Waterside Shops. Over the last month, a team of thieves had stormed the handbag department twice, making off with thirty-two bags each time.

Miami had experienced the same caper, and we were certain it was the same gang. Targeting only the priciest bags, it took four thieves under a minute to grab eight Chanel and Prada bags each. Saks was taking a seventy-thousand-dollar retail value hit each time. Who said crime wasn't scalable?

Vargas and I were set up in Waterside's security office watching video feeds. Two women officers, outfitted as sales ladies, patrolled the handbag department. Two officers milled around each of the exits, and two others sat idling in unmarked cars in the parking lot.

It was a waiting game, and though it was my operation, I was more interested in a twenty-five-year-old homicide than in nailing pocketbook crooks. I radioed the squad sergeant covering the entrance to the mall.

"Bill, it's Luca. I need you to manage this from the security office. Vargas and I have to see a witness in a homicide investigation."

* * *

Betty Kennedy lived in Egret's Walk, a coach-home community in Pelican Marsh. I loved the location of the Marsh, and it's four entrances provided great access. I considered this place myself and would have settled into one if they had two-car garages.

Kennedy's second-floor unit backed up to a lake where a fountain sprayed a huge volume of v-shaped water. I never liked fountains in lakes. Unless you had road noise to cover, they were kitschy.

Kennedy answered the door wearing crisp white jeans, a royal-blue blouse, and a smile. The modern interior belied her age and the unit's traditional exterior. She had glassed in the lanai overlooking the lake, extending her living space. I nudged Vargas, throwing a chin toward a cool treatment on a main wall. It was something I'd love to do in our place.

The kitchen was off-white with gray quartz countertops. We sat around a table made from the same material, which was overkill.

Kennedy said, "Can I get you something to drink?"

Mary Ann was on my back about not drinking enough, so I said, "A water would be nice."

"I'll take one too."

She opened the stainless fridge, handed off bottles, and sat.

Vargas said, "Thanks. We appreciate you coming forward with information."

"I have to be honest, when my sister told me, I was stunned. I didn't know what to do."

Vargas said, "You made the right decision."

I said, "Sister? Why don't you tell us what you know, Mrs. Kennedy?"

Kennedy picked at her sleeve and said, "My sister Cheryl, she just passed away two weeks ago. She had a bad case of cirrhosis of the liver. It wasn't from drinking or anything like that. She somehow contracted a viral type of hepatitis. They said it could have been from a needle when she was hospitalized after a car crash twenty years ago." Her eyes narrowed. "But that man she married, I think he was playing around with prostitutes and brought it home to Cheryl."

I said, "What's your sister's full name?"

"Cheryl Mackay."

Mackay? Pretty sure that was one of the people near the crime scene.

Jotting down the name, Vargas said, "Please continue."

"Cheryl was very sick. It was terrible; she was dying a little each day. It was so sad."

Kennedy hung her head, and Vargas patted her hand.

"Two days before she died, she was in hospice at home and very weak. I was with her constantly. I could feel that she wanted to tell me something. I tried to keep talking to her about when we were kids, you know, to distract her."

I said, "What did she tell you regarding the Boyle murder?"

"She said her husband, Lew, did it. That she lied to protect him."

"Lied about what?"

"After it happened, there were reports that Lew was seen in the area. He was a suspect and questioned. But Cheryl said he was with her when the murder happened, so they let him go."

"Your sister lied about his alibi?"

"Yes. She said she felt bad all these years about lying."

"How did the subject of Debbie Boyle's murder come up?"

"She knew she was going and wanted to get right with God. I called in Father Ahearn to hear her confession. After he left, she said there was something she had to get off her chest, and that's when she told me. Believe me, I was shocked. I asked her the next day to be sure, and she said she had lied to help Lew. Believe me, I never liked Lew, but I didn't think he'd do anything like killing that poor girl."

"What can you tell us about Lew, her husband?"

Kennedy scrunched her nose like she'd smelled a piece of bad fish. "He was beneath her. He's a crude man. Never treated Cheryl right."

"What does he do for a living?"

"Works for the county park system."

Vargas said, "Has he ever been violent?"

"I didn't see him much until she got sick. He made some very inappropriate comments to me."

"Can you share what he said?"

"No, but I'll tell you they were suggestive and lewd."

"Did he cheat on your sister?"

"Yes."

"Are you sure?"

"Absolutely. Cheryl told me about one of his affairs, and I told her she should leave him. She didn't want to, and we had a big argument about it. Believe me, I told her she was a fool to stay with him. After that, she never said anything more about him being unfaithful. You ask me, she was protecting him, didn't want to tell me."

"Did he like younger women?"

Kennedy smirked. "Show me a man who doesn't."

I said, "Did Lew Mackay have any history of going for very young girls, teenagers?"

"Can't say I would know that. I would think he'd keep that a secret."

"Did you ever see him staring at a younger girl? Or being friendly? Anything that seemed harmless at the time?"

She pulled her lips in and slowly shook her head. "I really can't say."

Vargas said, "That's okay." She held out a card. "Give it some more thought and call us with anything you remember."

We hopped in our Jeep Grand Cherokee and headed to see Lew Mackay.

"We nail Mackay for this, Chester should give us an office with a view of the Gulf."

"Don't pack yet, Frank. All we have is a hearsay deathbed confession. We don't have a stitch of evidence."

"We keep our heads down and do the work, we'll get the evidence."

"This is twenty-five years old, with twenty-five-year-old evidence and memories."

"I know it makes it tougher, but you know what? In all my years, up in Jersey and here, I never had a case go cold."

"Why am I getting the feeling you found your next obsession?"

"I don't like the way the case was handled."

"How can you say that? You just started looking into this today."

"I can't tell you why. I just know, that's all."

"All right, Frank. I'll go along for the ride, but you have to promise as soon as we start chasing ghosts, we back off."

"Deal. But don't forget, we have nothing but the pocketbook ring."

"You gonna tell the sheriff about this?"

"Let's see what this Mackay guy has to say first."

Chapter 4

"I really like this Cherokee, Mary Ann. Maybe when your lease is up you should get one."

"You know I'm not an SUV type of girl, Frank."

"You'll like it. You're up high, so you can see everything."

Turning off Livingston, I made a right into Delasol, a small community of single-family houses, where Lew Mackay lived. I had never looked seriously in here but knew they had limited amenities, which meant nice, low fees.

Mackay lived on Vallecas Lane, in a small Mediterranean styled home I pegged at five hundred thousand.

Hair thinning, Lew Mackay's face had a pinched look, like he'd banged a knee. Pale skinned, he didn't appear to spend time outdoors, which made me wary. Was he one of those people who carried an umbrella around to shield the sun? I didn't like him, even though he hadn't opened his mouth yet.

Mackay blinked as Vargas introduced us and stepped aside. A pile of sympathy cards and a white Bible bearing a red cross sat on the foyer's credenza.

Vargas said, "We're sorry for your loss, Mr. Mackay."

"Thank you. It's probably for the better; Cheryl was in a lot of pain."

"It's always difficult."

He sighed. "I know. Let's sit in the kitchen."

We followed him into a kitchen with oak cabinets topped with an even darker brown granite. There was an uncomfortable weight to the kitchen. I couldn't figure if the heaviness came from the recent death or from the hideous color scheme.

Mackay removed a wilting vase of flowers from the kitchen table and we settled into chairs.

Vargas said, "We've reopened the Deborah Boyle case."

Mackay's eyebrows lifted. "Really?"

I said, "Yes, in fact, it was your wife who precipitated the opening."

"My wife? What's Cheryl's death got to do with that?"

"She spoke to her sister, Betty Kennedy, shortly before she died."

"So? Betty was here every day."

"It seems your wife admitted that she had lied to the police about your alibi."

"My alibi?"

"The one she gave about your whereabouts the night Debbie Boyle was murdered."

"What? That I was home with her that night?"

"Exactly. She told her sister that was a lie, and that you weren't home with her."

He shrugged. "Look, now that she's gone I can tell you the truth. I was out with another woman that night."

Vargas said, "Okay, I can see why you wouldn't want your wife to know that."

"I feel terrible about being unfaithful, especially now."

I said, "Who was the woman?"

"Uh, I don't remember."

"You don't remember the woman you were with the night you were accused of murder? Come on now, who was the woman?"

"Her husband would go crazy."

"You should have considered that at the time. Name?"

His shoulders sagged. "Okay, I'll tell you what I was really doing. It was stupid, but a guy I knew, well, he dealt drugs, and he needed someone to meet a supplier down at Wiggins. I didn't touch the drugs or nothing. I just dropped off the money."

"How much money?"

"I don't know. I just handed off a bag; it wasn't that big."

"Who was this guy?"

"Ah, just some friend of a friend."

Vargas said, "We're going to need a name."

"I don't even know if he's around here anymore. Haven't seen him since."

I said, "You going to give up the name or not?"

"Hector Machado."

I jotted the name down. "And what's his last known address?"

"I don't know where he lived."

"Where did you supposedly meet him?"

"The old Pewter Mug, on forty-one."

"Dealing in drugs. That's a helluva new alibi you got there."

Vargas said, "How well did you know Debbie Boyle?"

"I—I didn't know her at all."

"Are you sure about that?"

"Absolutely. I swear. I never saw the kid."

"Okay, Mr. Mackay, that's enough for today."

The door closed behind us. I said, "Look at that sky, will you. Not a cloud in sight."

"Nice day. What did you think of Mackay?"

Shrugging, I dangled the keys. "You want to drive?"

Vargas eyed the Cherokee and frowned. "Nah."

"You're missing out."

"Maybe later."

"All right, we'll check on this Machado and see if narcotics knows if there was any noise on the Pewter back when this happened."

* * *

Since the crazy Aquatic Assassin case, things in Collier County had gone back to typically quiet. I couldn't figure out why Sheriff Chester seemed guarded when I greeted him.

"Take a seat, Frank."

"Thanks for seeing me, Sheriff. Don't worry, there's nothing crazy going on. Just wanted to let you know what I'm working on."

He didn't smile. "That's good."

"There was a murder, twenty-five years ago, down at Delnor-Wiggins Park. A girl was at the park with her brother and her boyfriend. She went missing and was found dead the next morning."

"What was the victim's name?"

"Deborah Boyle. She was just seventeen years old."

Chester shook his head. "Terrible."

"The case went cold too quickly, in my opinion."

"We didn't have much of a serious crime department back then. Who handled it?"

"Detective Ernest Foster. He doesn't appear to have much homicide experience."

"You want to reopen it?"

"Yes, I received a call from a woman whose sister made a deathbed confession. She had lied about her husband's alibi."

"You think it's him?"

"I'm not sure at this point, but I can tell you, and I've got all the respect in the world for my fellow officers, but this was not only rushed, it was sloppy."

"I don't want this department disparaged. Make sure that not a word of how poorly you believe the case was handled gets out. You understand?"

"Absolutely, sir. I just want the family to feel like justice was served."

"That would be nice. Okay, go ahead and reopen it. I'd love to close an old one."

"Thanks, sir."

I started to get up when Chester said, "Hold on a minute. I have something I'd like to discuss."

I sank down. "Sure. What about?"

Chester put an arm on his desk. "You and Detective Vargas."

"Oh. What about?"

"You tell me. I'm aware of your relationship. I'm not passing judgment on it. In fact, I like Detective Vargas and think you make a nice couple."

I eked out a thanks and Chester continued, "This office has rules about interdepartmental relationships . . ."

"But we checked on it, sir. We were told that it only mattered if you were married."

"Married? That doesn't quite mean what it once did. There are all kinds of relationships these days, and legal believes the intent of the verbiage was to prevent compromising situations."

Legal? The sheriff was talking to damn lawyers about my relationship with Mary Ann?

"There is absolutely nothing to be concerned about, sir. We conduct ourselves with the highest level of integrity that—"

Chester threw up a palm. "Save it, Luca. It's out of my hands. You're cohabitating, and as such, cannot work the same shift together."

"So, it's either my girlfriend or my partner?"

"It's the perfect time to change partners." He knocked a knuckle on the desk. "We don't have a major crime on our hands."

"But we work so well together."

"You have a lot to offer, Frank. You'll train someone new."

"How long do we have?"

"No more than ninety days."

Chapter 5

The more I thought about it the madder I got. I was careful not to slam the door when I came in. The TV was on, and the smell of garlic was in the air. I headed to the kitchen.

Mary Ann was watching *WINK News* as she stirred a pot on the stove.

"What are you making?"

"Escarole and beans."

My favorite comfort food. How the hell did this woman know I was upset?

"What's the matter, Frank?"

"What are you, some kind of witch?"

"You going to tell me?"

"Chester's splitting us up. He's giving us ninety days to wind it down."

"We had to expect it, Frank. Why are you surprised?"

"I'm not surprised. I'm pissed. You realize I'm losing my partner for the second time?"

"Take it easy. This is totally different." She wrapped her arms around me. "I'm still here. I'll always be here for you."

"But don't you care?"

"I care, but honestly, it's better this way. We'll be able to separate our work lives from the rest of our lives."

"But I don't want to do that. I like working with you."

"So do I, Frank, but trust me, it's better this way."

* * *

After Mary Ann went to sleep, I grabbed a file and a bottle of water and retreated to the lanai. A big fat moon was sitting on the tree line, casting a yellow glow onto the pool. I cracked open the water, thinking that with the quiet vibe and postcard scene I should have made coffee instead.

Brian Boyle, the seven-year-old brother of the victim, had been interviewed three times. The first time his mother was present, and the interview was conducted by Detective Foster at the Boyle household. It took place the afternoon the body was discovered and wasn't recorded. Witnessing the questioning was a uniformed officer named Henry Glevek. Foster's signature appeared below his summary:

> The witness, Brian Boyle, is a minor. He accompanied his sister to Delnor-Wiggins Pass Park the night of May 14, 1993. They drove to the park in Wheeler's car. The witness is uncertain what time they arrived but said it was still light out when they arrived. The park is open from sunrise to two hours after sundown, which was appx. 8:07 p.m.
>
> The mother of both Brian and Debbie Boyle confirmed she had attended a wedding that night, a Friday, and left Debbie to care for Brian.
>
> Witness states that the victim's boyfriend, John Wheeler, was also present and brought along one or two duffel bags. Arriving at the beach, the victim spread out a blanket and they sat on it. They played cards and ate sandwiches the victim had brought from home. They walked by the water and held hands.
>
> The witness said there were other people walking by the water but could not identify anyone. He said someone was fishing from the beach but could not estimate the distance. When pressed, the witness could not be certain it was a male nor that he or she was actually fishing.
>
> Sometime after dark, the three of them were laying on the blanket, looking at the stars when his sister left

to go to the bathroom. He is uncertain where she intended to go but based upon the witness's recollection, headed in a northern direction.

After a period, unknown in length, the boyfriend got up and told the witness to stay on the blanket, he was going to find out where the victim was. After an indeterminate period of time, the witness left the blanket and carried one of two lanterns with him to the water's edge. He thought the couple might be taking a walk.

The witness ran into Clem Walker, who claimed to be fishing at the time. The witness and Walker walked toward the direction that the witness came from and met John Wheeler.

The witness said that Mr. Wheeler had a bruise on his forehead, was excited and yelling. The three of them searched for some time but couldn't find his sister. He was unsure who recommended they call the police.

I put the report down. Young children like Brian Boyle were unable to gauge the passage of time. The kid's inability to determine when his sister had left and how long she and Wheeler were gone contributed to the depth of the rabbit hole. But the main question I had was about the supposed wound Wheeler had suffered. He was knocked out but was able to search for Debbie Boyle and drive home? What did the fisherman have to say about the injury?

The second interview was conducted two days later, on May seventeenth. It was conducted by Detective Foster in his office. Brian Boyle's mother was not present, but the proceedings were recorded. Scanning the transcript, I eyed where the meat was:

> Foster - When you were sitting on the blanket, what was your sister and John Wheeler doing?
>
> Boyle - We were playing Steal the Old Man's Bundle.

Foster - Boyfriends and girlfriends like to kiss each other. Were your sister and her boyfriend kissing?

Brian - I think a little.

Foster - Girlfriends like when their boyfriends touch them. Did Johnnie touch Debbie?

Brian - I don't know.

Foster - Think. Were they sitting close together?

Brian - Yes.

Foster - Was Debbie giggling? She liked Johnnie, didn't she?

Brian - Yes.

Foster - So, she liked it when Johnnie touched her.

Brian - Yes.

Foster - Your sister and Johnnie were together a lot, weren't they?

Brian - Yes.

Foster - Johnnie is a nice guy but like all people, even your mother, he would get mad at times, right?

Brian - Sometimes he would get mad at me.

Foster - And he would get mad at Debbie, right?

Brian - Yes.

Foster - And they would fight sometimes.

Brian - Sometimes.

Foster - Did Debbie leave the blanket to get away from Johnnie?

Brian - She said she had to go to the bathroom.

Foster - Sometimes adults say things they don't mean.

You know that, don't you?

Brian - Yes.

Foster - It could be that she left to get away from Johnnie, right?

Brian - I guess.

Foster - When Debbie left to get away from Johnnie, did Johnnie follow her?

Brian - No.

Foster - Are you sure? Couldn't you have been distracted? Playing with cards and missed him following after her?

I couldn't read anymore. Foster was steering the kid. This wouldn't pass the smell test with a judge, no less a defense attorney.

Wheeler's story was tough to believe, but Foster was building a case against him that would collapse in a courtroom. It made no sense.

Flipping to the end, I shook my head. Foster hadn't signed it. This guy was grating on me.

The third interview was more of the same —useless. If the family knew how poorly the inquiry into the crime was handled they'd go to the press or file a lawsuit. It was up to me to conduct a proper investigation and bring the killer to justice.

Chapter 6

The news that Foster wasn't a homicide detective strengthened my feeling I was onto something. The force was a lot smaller back then, and the one and only detective with homicide experience had been recovering from a hip transplant. For Detective Foster, who normally handled burglaries, the Boyle case was his first homicide.

Who was the sheriff back in 1993? Whoever it was blew it. He should have gotten help from another county and run a proper investigation. It was terrible but something I was confident I could fix.

Pumped that I'd be able to solve a cold one, I headed to see John Wheeler, who sat at the top of my list of suspects.

Wheeler had stuck to his story during numerous interviews. He claimed to have gone looking for Debbie Boyle after she'd been missing twenty minutes. Wheeler insisted they were not fighting and that she went to the bathroom.

He said he walked from their blanket, which was about fifty feet from the water's edge, through a treed area, providing cover for a picnic area, toward the bathroom. As he approached the building, he heard a sound, and when he turned, was hit by something and collapsed.

He stated that when he regained consciousness he went to find Brian, who was with Clem Walker. They then went looking for Debbie, spending half an hour before Wheeler insisted they get the police involved.

* * *

If Wheeler was assaulted, and it was a big if, I wondered if Clem Walker had enough time to attack both Boyle and Wheeler and make it back to the beach. Who knows, maybe he was looking to do the kid in too.

***

It was a perfect day, with zero humidity and a bright, warm sun. It was mid-November, and I was looking forward to at least six months of incredible weather. I left my sunglasses on the dashboard and walked to the door of Wheeler's one-story home.

Wheeler lived in Vasari, a community named after the Italian artist Giorgio Vasari. It was in Bonita Springs, along the Naples border. It was a nice neighborhood, but it was a bundled community, meaning you paid for golf whether you played or not. Why did people who never golfed live in bundled communities?

His Mediterranean house was dark beige, like all the others, carrying the uniformity edict into boredom land. Walking to the door, I heard someone practicing the trumpet. I kicked a palm frond aside and rang the bell.

John Wheeler came to the door holding a can of root beer. His black hair was wet and combed straight back. He looked much younger than the forty-seven he was.

"Mr. Wheeler? Detective Frank Luca."

"Good to meet you."

We shook hands. His were beefy and sandpapery. I pegged him as a plumber.

There were a handful of toy trucks in the living area that led to a small, screen-enclosed pool. The yard backed up to a mangy preserve. A female voice floated in from a hallway, cajoling a kid to take a bath.

I followed Wheeler through the open sliders to a fiberglass table. The spa's spillover covered most of the trumpet player's screeching.

"Nice place you have here."

"Thanks, we bought it right, about five years ago, before things got moving again."

"What do you do for a living?"

"Electrician."

Close. "You get to play a lot of golf?"

"My wife does. I get out maybe twice a month. You play?"

"Not yet. Maybe one of these days I'll pick it up."

He laughed. "You better have patience. It can get frustrating."

"It's what keeps me from trying." I took out my Moleskine. "I wanted to ask you about the night Debbie Boyle was murdered."

Wheeler frowned and leaned on the table. "It was a long time ago, but it seems like yesterday in some respects."

He fed me the perfect response. "A call came in recently, and we've reopened the case." Wheeler didn't flinch at the news, but my request to see him had put him on guard. "I have a couple of questions."

He guzzled the last of the root beer. "Sure."

"What time did you get to the park that night?"

"A little before seven."

"Did you see many people there?"

He began to pulse squeeze the empty can of soda, making an annoying clicking sound, "There were quite a few people. You know, people walking the beach, a couple of people fishing. It was a nice night, full moon, if I remember, so people came out."

"Did you ever hit Debbie Boyle?"

"What? Of course not. I've never hit a woman in my life. What kind of man do you think I am?"

"I'm not questioning your manhood, but you were a kid at the time you were dating her."

"Younger, yes, but no kid, I was twenty-two."

"There was a report that you and Debbie took off, leaving Brian alone, to have a little private time."

Wheeler crushed the can. "That's bullshit. We had plenty of opportunities to be, ah, intimate. Besides, she never would leave her brother alone. Debbie was a very responsible girl."

"Do you think it's responsible to take a seven-year-old to the beach at night?"

"We weren't doing anything crazy. The kid was perfectly safe. He had the two of us looking after him. We'd never let anything happen to him."

"When you went looking for Debbie, you went alone, right?"

"Yes."

"But you left Brian alone when you did."

He shrugged. "I guess so."

"What do you mean, you guess so? You did. You left a seven-year-old boy alone, in the dark, in a strange place."

"Wiggins ain't no strange place, he'd been there tons of times."

"Why didn't you take him with you to look for her?"

"I don't know. I just thought I could check on her faster. A seven-year-old doesn't move that fast, you know. My boy is almost seven, and he gets distracted easily."

"Would you leave your son alone on a beach."

"No. Of course not."

"I thought so. That's why it's hard to understand why you left Brian alone that night. Were you doing anything else irresponsible that night, like drinking or taking drugs?"

"No. Neither of us took any drugs, and we didn't drink much."

A couple of empty beer cans were found near the place they had set up, and though there was a small amount of alcohol in the victim's blood, no one had said Wheeler acted or smelled drunk.

"When you got to the beach, how did you decide where to set up?"

"Uh, I think Brian had something to do with it. He ran right down to the water, and we kinda of backed up from there."

"Who decided to stop looking for Debbie and call the police?"

"I did. I was panicking, you know. I felt like time was running out. If someone took her, the faster the police could find her . . ."

"But why didn't you just take off?"

"We did."

"But you went back and picked up the blanket and all your belongings."

"It only took a second." He threw up his hands, adding, "I had to get my flip-flops anyway."

"Your sworn statements claim that you went looking around before going by the bathrooms."

"That's right. I zigzagged around the area behind where we were and then went to where the bathrooms were."

"She said she was going to the bathroom. Why didn't you go straight to the bathroom to look for her?"

"The bathrooms get locked up at sunset."

Good answer, except, "But back in 1993 the locks on the bathroom building nearest to you had been busted."

"I always took a piss behind the trees whenever we went."

"Did you go to the park often?"

"Yeah, I went a lot. It was a great place to hang out."

"With all the time you spent there, you would think you'd know the bathroom locks were busted off."

"Like I said, it was no big deal, I took my leaks by the trees."

"Getting back to your search for Debbie. You were near the bathrooms when you heard something and say you were struck?"

"I didn't *say*. I *was* struck." He jabbed a finger into his forehead. "Right here."

"What made you turn around?"

"I don't know. It was a little windy that night, and I can't be sure if I heard something or if it was like a sixth sense, you know, when you can feel there's somebody there."

"Was it male or female who you believe struck you?"

"I don't know. I'd think it was a man because of the strength factor. I was knocked out."

"You fell to the ground?"

"Yes, a total collapse."

"Can you explain why you had no other injuries beside the forehead wound?"

"What are you talking about? I got smacked in the head with a bar or a piece of wood and was knocked out."

"When someone is knocked unconscious, oftentimes they get bruised when they fall since they can't protect themselves. You know, hit their face, arms, legs, that sort of thing."

"It was on sand; it was soft, so it probably helped."

"No abrasions from the sand?"

He shook his head. "None."

"When you came to, what did you do?"

"I was disoriented, didn't know where I was. It took me a couple seconds for the fog to lift. Then I ran to Brian."

"You didn't look anymore for Debbie?"

"No. I was worried about Brian."

We danced around a bit. I couldn't figure if he was hiding something or if he was looking to polish his reputation. I didn't like the story; it was way too convenient. Hit hard enough to get knocked out but not badly injured? I was going to go over Wheeler closer than a proctologist would.

Chapter 7

As soon as Vargas came in, I tossed a file onto her desk. "We got to take a look at Clem Walker. The case file portrays this guy more like a Good Samaritan than a suspect."

"That's the guy who was fishing, right?"

"Yep, and if Foster challenged Walker's version of events, it's not evident in the file."

"Unusual. Maybe they cleared him somehow."

"Be honest with me if you think this is another miscue, or am I judging the handling of this case too harshly?"

"Skepticism is an Olympic sport for you, Frank. But there's no doubt. The way this appears to have been handled raises questions."

"I mean, was it a coincidence that Walker was close to the kid after the girl and Wheeler went missing? Or was he involved in some way? Check out what I ran on him. This Walker's got a shady past."

"Hmm, I don't know, just a couple of marijuana arrests, petty theft—"

I slammed a palm on my desk. "He assaulted his next-door neighbor, for Chrissakes!"

"Take it easy, Frank. I thought you were focused on Wheeler."

"There's a list of characters that need to be reexamined, and who knows what Foster missed? We have to approach this like it happened yesterday."

"Okay, but it's not going to be easy. Whatever evidence there is, it's a quarter century old. Between that and the faded memories, it's going to be tough."

"No doubt time erodes your memory, but certain things remain crystal clear, especially when it's connected to the murder of someone you knew or something traumatic. We all remember what we were doing when those bastards flew the planes into the World Trade Center. You don't forget things like that; it gets seared into your brain."

"I know you're right, but I'm just saying…"

"Look, the reality is no case is easy."

"Don't you think I realize that? I don't know what you're all worked up about."

I pointed to a white board capped with Debbie Boyle's picture. "What am I worked up about? That poor girl, who was only seventeen years old. Her and her mother. It's small consolation, but we have a responsibility to see that justice is done and someone is held accountable. I've got a feeling we're gonna be able to fix that. The thought that some killer got away with it and is out there laughing at us burns the shit out of me."

"We'll get him if we can, Frank."

"Something is in this one, Vargas. I can feel it. I know you're gonna say I always say that, but it's different this time."

* * *

Clem Walker lived in a small home on Capri Island, a tiny island just before the bridge to Marco Island. Italy it wasn't. A boat and a red pickup were in the driveway of the sky-blue home.

The front door was open and voices from a TV game show bled through the screen door. The bell had a lame ring to it. I hit it twice. A chair scraped, and cigarette in hand, Walker came into view.

Walker was deeply tanned, his faced lined and leathery. His T-shirt hugged his lean frame, it's logo unreadable.

"Mr. Walker? Detective Luca."

The screen door creaked open. "Come on in. You want a beer?"

"No thanks, I'm on duty."

The house had no air-conditioning, but two fans in the main room kept it comfortable. We settled around a kitchen table. The place had a dialed-down fish market smell to it.

Walker snuffed out his cigarette in the shell he used as an ashtray. "So, after all these years, you're looking into that kid's murder?"

"New information surfaced on the case."

"You're gonna be able to catch the guy?"

"I think so."

"What changed?"

"Can't discuss it, but it's material. I have a couple of questions for you."

Walker shifted in his chair, tapping another cigarette out of a pack. "Sure."

"What were you doing on the beach that night Boyle was murdered?"

"Fishing."

"Where exactly?"

"I can't tell you exactly. I walk the beach, casting and reeling."

"How long were you out there?"

"Two hours or so."

"When you ran into the kid, Brian Boyle, where were you?"

"Geez, I don't know exactly. I saw the kid walking by the water. He was alone, and I walked toward him."

"What did he say?"

"That his sister was lost, and he wanted to find her."

"How long after that did John Wheeler appear?"

"Not long. I asked him a couple of questions to be sure about the kid's sister and all. Then we started walking where the kid said they were."

"How far was that?"

"I didn't know where they were set up."

"But you said you were fishing up and down the beach for two hours. There was a full moon out that night. You must've seen where they were."

He hesitated before saying, "I saw them once, I'm pretty sure it was them."

"Who else had a kid out there that night?"

"Nobody I saw."

"When Wheeler approached you, what was your impression of him?"

Walker's cigarette glowed red as he took a pull. "He was jumpy, nervous, kinda out of breath. He was talking fast, saying he was attacked by somebody."

"Did you notice his bruise?"

"Yeah, his forehead was red and bleeding a little."

"Did you notice if a bump had formed?"

"I think so. Nothing crazy, but you could tell something hit his head."

"What did you do then?"

"We went looking for the missing girl."

"Where did you look?"

"We went to their blanket. I asked him what direction she went in, and we went that way."

"Did you split up?"

"No, we stayed together."

"Why? You could have covered more ground going separate ways."

"I guess. Look, things were crazy. A girl was missing, and this guy said he was attacked, and we had a kid with us."

"How long did you look around?"

"About a half an hour, and then I said we got to call the police."

"You're the one who suggested calling the police?"

"Yeah."

"Was Wheeler wearing anything on his feet when you were looking for Debbie Boyle?"

"His feet? Uh, I think he had flip-flops on. Yeah, I'm pretty sure he did."

"I just have one more question for you. You said you were out fishing, right?"

"Yeah."

"What kind of fish were you going for?"

"There's all kinds out there. Sometimes you can bag snapper, pig fish, sand sharks. One time I even caught a cobia."

"How come you didn't have a bucket with you?"

There was a perceptible sag to his shoulders. "You sure about that?"

"Absolutely."

"It was a long while ago; I don't remember. Besides, a lot of times

I just go out and fish for the sport of it. It keeps me calm."

I got up to leave and said, "Really? You drive all the way to Wiggins to fish, at night? There must be plenty of fish around this island."

Chapter 8

There was a knock on the door, and I buried my face behind my monitor. Vargas rolled away from her desk and headed to the door. "Frank, he's here."

It was really happening. Derrick Dickson was going to be my new partner. I'd met the six-foot redhead in the sheriff's office a week ago. The thirty-two-year-old had come down to paradise from a ratty suburb outside of DC. The young detective had decent experience with gangs, sex rings, and drugs. The problem was we didn't have much of that down in Collier County. I pushed back and stood.

"How you doing, Derrick?"

He set down one of his backpacks and we shook hands. "Good, sir. Anxious to get started."

I couldn't muster a me too, but Vargas said, "We'll share my desk for the time being. I'm moving upstairs."

"You sure? I don't want to be a bother."

"No problem. I'm not going to be in here much anyway."

I said, "Homicide's a lot different than dealing with a drug ring. It can get squeamish. You have a strong stomach?"

"Yes, sir. My father used to say I had a cast-iron one."

I wanted to test him right then and there and pull out a couple of pictures of decomposing bodies and see if he'd barf.

Vargas said, "You'll be fine. He's just trying to scare you."

"What are you working on now, sir?"

I said, "A cold case. Call came in on a twenty-five-year-old case, where a young girl was stabbed to death at Delnor-Wiggins Park."

Vargas said, "Detective Luca received a call, claiming they had information to solve the murder."

"What kind of information?"

I said, "We'll get to all that. You unload your bags, and then we'll start."

"Sounds good."

"And Derrick, around here we like to dress professionally. I don't know what they do in Washington, but down here it's suits and ties."

Vargas stepped out to the bathroom, and Derrick was whistling as he settled in. I wanted to stick pictures of Debbie Boyle's body under his nose to stop the whistling but cooled my instincts.

Spreading a dozen photos across my desk, I asked, "Look at these pictures. What do you see?"

Vargas walked back in as Derrick bent over, his nose inches from the collage of crime scene photos. "It's a crime scene."

"What tipped you off, the yellow tape?"

Vargas shot me a bone-chilling stare and I softened.

"Look closely at the investigators themselves. Do you notice anything about them?"

Derrick stood up, a bead of perspiration hanging off his upper lip, and shook his head. "I'm sorry, I see detectives and uniformed officers at the scene. They seem to be searching the area."

"Look at their hands, their feet."

Derrick picked up two of the photos and examined them. "I give up."

"First off, we don't give up in homicide. You think the poor families who lost a loved one would want us to give up?"

"No, sir."

"Secondly, and I do hope you're a quick learner, the crime scene is contaminated."

"How can you tell by looking at photographs?"

"No one is wearing gloves, booties, or heaven forbid, forensic coveralls. They're tramping around out there destroying footprints, dropping hairs, fibers, and who knows what else."

"But this case is twenty-five years old, right? They probably didn't know any better."

"Bullshit. Forensics wasn't what it is today, but they blew the fundamentals. Cops have been putting people away on hairs and fibers forever."

"I remember at the academy, they said DNA was first used in the late eighties."

Vargas said, "I think the first case DNA was used in court was in 1984."

I said, "This woman is incredible. Derrick, if you can be half as good as her, you'll be a damn good detective."

Vargas smiled. "You'll be fine. I'm really not that good, but whatever I know, Detective Luca taught me."

She didn't know I was panicking as each day passed, bringing me closer to losing my backup. She'd saved my ass so many times I stopped counting. Was my memory bad from the chemo I took for my bladder cancer, or had I been getting lazy, realizing I had Vargas to backstop me?

Derrick said, "I'll try my best."

Vargas said, "Ask as many questions as necessary. Don't be afraid. Detective Luca will be patient with you, right, Frank?"

"Sure."

"Don't let him intimidate you, Derrick. It's all a show. He's really a teddy bear. I gotta go up to HR. I'll see you boys later."

Since Chester set the sun on our professional relationship, we began taking two cars to the office. I brought Derrick up to speed on the Boyle case, coloring the interviews I conducted with Wheeler, Walker, and Mackay with my suspicions. My new partner had a couple of solid questions but not the magical insight Vargas seemed to deliver. It was six o'clock, and time to go home. I said, "We're going to see a witness or two tomorrow, so lay off the booze tonight and be ready to go at nine."

"Okay, no problem. You mind if I stay and read the Boyle case file?"

"That's a good idea, just don't stay too late."

* * *

The salmon fillet and shrimp skewers I'd picked up at Publix were on the grill before Mary Ann's garage door was down.

"Smells good. You want a glass of wine?"

"Sure. I bought a couple of a bottles from Provence."

"You just love saying Provence, don't you? That's really why you got them."

"No, I remember Barnet saying they produce good Grenache and they're not expensive. Get one; I put them in the closet."

Vargas came out with two glasses of dark purple wine and handed me one.

"Salute."

We touched glasses. I took a sniff of the inky wine and sipped. It was dark tasting, like blackberries,

"What do you think? I like it."

"I don't know, it seems a bit heavy for seafood."

"Barnet said Grenache goes with everything."

"He could have, except this isn't Grenache."

"How could that be?"

"The label said it was Syrah, Mr. Connoisseur."

"It was in the Grenache section, and I just thought . . ."

"No big deal. I like it. How long till the fish is ready?"

* * *

While clearing the table, Mary Ann said, "Derrick seems like a good choice as your partner."

"Really? He's green as grass."

"You're good at training someone. Look what you did with me, you moved yourself into my house."

"What do you mean by that?"

"Nothing, Frank. It's a joke, okay?"

I forced a smile. "He stayed tonight to read the case file. He seems okay, but how the hell did he miss the fact that those dinosaurs were trampling the Boyle crime scene?"

"This was his first day. He was nervous."

"What's he got to be nervous about?"

"Frank, you may not realize it, but at times you can be intimidating. You don't like to be challenged."

"What's that supposed to mean?"

"You like to lead. You don't want to be questioned."

"That's bullshit. You really believe that? Is that the way I treated you?"

"No, no. Not me. We worked great together, but sometimes you can be short with people."

"If someone is being an asshole, I got no time for that."

"Sometimes we have to deal with people we'd rather not, but we still have to. That's when you have to find a way to keep cool. It makes no sense to piss anyone off. Listen to them and smile. It works, trust me."

"I do that a lot with the sheriff and his bureaucrats."

"I know. Now you have to do the same with people down the line."

"Why'd they have to screw things up and split us up? We worked great together. I'll bet they'll have to hire another detective to make up for what we did together."

"Nothing stays the same, Frank. Change is the only constant."

"Maybe, but I'm telling you this isn't good for the department. Next tough case we get and Chester starts beating my ass up for a solve, I'm going to throw this back at him."

The thought of losing someone who could fill in my blanks was scaring the hell out of me. Mary Ann protected me when I had a lapse in memory. It wasn't that I couldn't function without her as a partner. It was that she knew my flaws and kept them to herself. That protection was disappearing like a Florida rain shower, and I didn't like the damn feel of it.

Chapter 9

Derrick was early, which was good, but he was outfitted in a light beige suit. It was November, for God's sake. Northerners never realized Florida also had seasons. If someone was wearing white pants in the winter you could bet they were either a vacationer or newly transplanted.

He'd picked up coffee for me, a nice gesture, but it had way too much milk in it. I'd make sure he never made that mistake again and left it in on my desk untouched. We talked over the case as we drove, and I told him three times his role was observatory.

The Dunes were a collection of luxury high-rises in North Naples that bordered the entrance to Delnor-Wiggins Park. They weren't beachfront, but those apartments lucky enough to face west had stunning Gulf views.

A twelve-story building called Antigua was where Diane Nielsen called home. As soon as she opened the door to her seventh-floor condo, I smelled burnt toast. A TV in the kitchen was blaring an annoying morning show.

The sliders' plantation shutters were open, and the view of a bay with green mangroves melting into the Gulf was mesmerizing.

Somewhere around sixty, Nielsen was an energetic bird of a woman. "It's nice, isn't it?"

"For sure. It'd be hard to get me off that deck."

Nielsen laughed a bit too hard. The string of pearls around her neck was a giveaway she had looked forward to our talk. I'd have to be careful she didn't embellish or keep us too long. I took a glance around, not as open as I expected. It probably was one of the first buildings built in the Dunes.

"Can I get you boys some coffee?"

I said, "Absolutely. If you don't mind, I'd like a tiny splash of milk, nothing more. How about you, Detective Dickson?"

"Thank you, ma'am, but I'm fine."

As a Keurig buzzed, I breezed to the sliders past a credenza covered with pictures of her grandchildren. It could have been the vantage point or lack of glare, but the Gulf appeared supersized.

Nielsen set a cup and saucer on a glass table with a liver-spotted hand. "Here you are, Detective Luca. Is the amount of milk okay?"

The coffee was chestnut brown. "Perfect. People usually put too much milk in, but you got it right."

"My husband was like that. He hated too much milk and despised cream in coffee."

Sounds like my kind of man, except I was guessing he wasn't walking around anymore. She disappeared into the kitchen and came out with two bottles of water. We sat around the table and I said, "As I mentioned, we've reopened the Deborah Boyle case."

"That's good. I was upset that no one was ever charged."

Derrick chimed in, "We're working hard to change that, ma'am."

Eyebrows raised, I nodded at him. "While reviewing the files and statement you gave, we had further questions that could help move the case forward."

Nielsen smiled like she was on a game show. "It'd be my pleasure to help."

"What were you doing on the beach that night?"

"Talking a walk. I promised myself before we moved here that if was lucky enough to live by the beach, that I'd make it my business to take a walk each night. I've kept it up like I knew my Jack would want me to. You know, a lot of people feel they have to move when they lose their spouse . . ."

"What time were you there?"

"I usually go out before eight. I like to digest my dinner before I do any exercise. I feel it—"

"What specifically did you see that night?"

"It was a beautiful night. Full moon, a light breeze, perfect. There were a couple of other people out walking and a man was fishing. I think they call it surf fishing, but I don't think he caught anything."

"The man fishing, did he have a bucket or anything with him?"

Nielsen looked at the ceiling for a moment. "Hm, I don't think so. He had a fishing pole, that I remember, but nothing else, I don't believe. Is that okay?"

Derrick said, "That's fine, ma'am. What did he look like?"

"Oh, he was, like they say on the police shows, male, Caucasian, medium build—"

I said, "You mentioned seeing someone nearer to the path that leads to the entrance."

"Oh yes, it was a woman. She had blond hair."

"A woman? Are you sure?"

"I think so. It looked like a woman to me."

"I realize it's a long time ago, but your statement made no mention of a woman or anyone with blond hair, for that matter."

"I saw what I saw. It's not my fault if the detective didn't write it down, is it?"

Derrick said, "As long as you didn't withhold information. If you did, it could be considered obstruction."

I told this kid three times to keep his mouth shut. "You've got nothing to worry about, Mrs. Nielsen. What was this woman doing?"

"She seemed to be hiding, if you know what I mean."

No, I don't know what you mean. "Can you explain what this woman seemed to be doing?"

"She was close to the mangroves. I saw her the first time I passed. My peripheral vision is very good. Dr. Morton, he says it's one of the best he's seen—"

"What made you believe she was hiding?"

"When I looked in her direction she scooted out of sight. She did it both times I passed."

"So, you saw a medium-built woman—"

"She was bigger than medium for a woman."

"Okay. A larger framed woman, with blond hair. Was it long or short?"

"Long but not really long. When I was a kid, my hair was down to here, now look at me."

"How old would you guess this woman to have been?"

"I don't really know. But if I had to guess, I'd say twenty-five or thirty."

* * *

Before the elevator doors closed, Derrick said, "What do you think? Could it have been the girl?"

"What I think is, you don't listen. I asked you to observe today, not talk."

"But I did. I hardly said anything."

"What was that nonsense about what the fisherman looked like?"

"Isn't that important?"

"Did you read the file last night?"

"Yeah, why?"

"We had several witnesses that identified Clem Walker as the man fishing. You were wasting time."

"But there could be another guy who was fishing."

"Really? How come no one saw him?"

"But there was no mention of a woman being there like Mrs. Nielsen mentioned."

The kid had a point. "We don't know for sure it was a woman. But if it was, it opens another avenue to pursue."

"I know it's a stupid question, but why is that?"

"If you examined the pictures of Debbie Boyle, you would have noticed that she had numerous stab wounds on her face."

"Anger?"

"Close. It could be a girl who was jealous of Boyle. She was a good-looking kid. Maybe she was dating a woman's boyfriend and she wanted revenge, not only killing her but destroying her looks."

"What are we going to do?"

"Right now, we're going to see somebody that needs to be interviewed."

Chapter 10

It was time to do what I'd kept putting off—go see Debbie Boyle's mother. I was pissed that Vargas wouldn't come with me. She gave me the bullshit I'd have to do it without her sooner or later. Why couldn't it be later? Vargas was great with sympathy, while I had to force myself to express regrets. I didn't want emotion to screw with my instincts.

No way Derrick was coming with me. He was too young and green to understand how devastating the loss of a child was to a mother. Twenty-five years later, and the son said his mother was still struggling.

Cathy Boyle hadn't moved from the Carlton Lakes home she brought her kids up in. The beige ranch had a black door and a two-car garage that angled to the right. A circle of rose bushes were guarded by a pair of stone angels.

I don't know why I was surprised, but the victim's mother and her daughter could have passed as twins. Cathy Boyle's shoulder-length, blond hair even seemed to be cut the same way her daughter's had been. They had the same nose. The major difference was the younger Boyle had an athletic build, while her mother was thin and frail.

"Mrs. Boyle, it's nice to meet you."

She might be suffering, but her steely eyes sized me up. "I've been waiting a long time for something like this. Come on in."

The house was bright and neat but deafeningly quiet. There was a hint of Lemon Pledge in the air. We sat down in the family room on couches facing each other. The coffee table between us held three small family photos and a large picture of her daughter in a party dress.

"As I mentioned over the phone, your daughter's case has been reopened. I know you have questions about it, but be aware that I may be unable to discuss certain aspects."

"Do you finally have someone you believe is responsible?"

"We have new information on an individual that we're pursuing."

"Who is it?"

"I can't discuss that, ma'am."

"Why not? Someone killed my daughter."

"I understand, Mrs. Boyle, but it's preliminary in nature, and it wouldn't be fair to release information until we're certain."

"You're not certain, but you've reopened the case?"

"That's correct, ma'am. The new information prompted me to review the case file, and I'm taking a fresh look at everything."

She blinked. "Above and beyond the new information?"

"Yes. I want to be certain that everything is closely reexamined. You never know what you'll find with a new set of eyes."

"I knew it, the case was mishandled."

"All I can say at this point is that I'm reviewing the entire investigation. If and when something changes, I promise, you'll be the first to know."

She eyed me suspiciously. "I hope so, Detective. You have no idea how difficult this has been for me and my son."

She was right, and I sorely missed Vargas's touch. I wanted to run out of the room. "You're right, ma'am. I can't imagine the misery you've had to endure. I want to bring whoever did this to justice, and I promise I'm going to do my best to solve your daughter's death."

"My family deserves better. My children lost their father. After he passed, we picked up the pieces and recovered. When Debbie was taken, I lost the will to live. I went through the motions for Brian, but he deserved a better mother than I was able to be."

"You did the best you could, ma'am. And I'm going to do the same for you."

"I'm sorry to be so negative, but it's been twenty-five years since my baby was ripped out of my arms. I'm thankful, really I am, that you're looking into this."

"I'd like to ask you a couple of questions, background information that would help give me a picture of her."

"Of course. Debbie was special, so full of life and open to life itself. She loved to try new things, have new experiences. Debbie loved children and wouldn't hurt a fly." She stood. "Come, I'll show you her room. It'll give you a sense of who she was."

I was surprised and confused. The kid was dead twenty-five years, and the mother still kept a room for her?

She pointed out her son's room as we went down a hallway. "Here's Debbie's room."

Light flooded into the room from a half-moon window covered with sheers. It was a museum to the early nineties. There were posters of the New Kids on the Block band, Mariah Carey, and Guns N' Roses. This kid liked a wide range of music.

Scanning the room from the doorway, it seemed as if not a single thing had been put away. The dresser top had a contraption with a bunch of necklaces hanging off it, and there were picture frames, bracelets, and hairbrushes neatly lined up. A boom box sat on top of a nightstand, surrounded by stacks of cassette tapes.

Mrs. Boyle said, "That's where I nursed her and read to her every night." She pointed to a white rocking chair with a pink, checked cushion.

I backed into the hallway. "Thanks for showing me. Let's have a quick chat before I have to go."

When we sat back down she seemed energized.

"Okay, what would you like to know?"

"Any questions I ask are purely to help me. Please don't get offended."

"I've been dragged through the mud, called a terrible mother for letting my daughter and son go to the park in the first place. People blamed me. I was in therapy for two years. I know it wasn't my fault. I don't think you're going to upset me."

She was as resolved as she was ever going to be, so I might as well go straight at it. "Debbie lost a father at an early age. Most girls who do gravitate toward older men. Was that the case with Debbie?"

"It's possible that losing her father may have been the reason she seemed to like older boys, but Debbie was mature for her age. She was responsible beyond her years and intelligent."

"Her boyfriend, John Wheeler, was twenty-two at the time. I never had children, and I'm not passing judgment, but that seems like a large age difference."

"What's your point? I told you she was mature."

"What did you think of John Wheeler?"

She narrowed her eyes. "He was a nice young man and treated Debbie like the princess she was. Brian adored him. He never gave me a reason to doubt him, but his story never sat well with me. He left my son alone to look for Debbie? Why? He gets hit on the head and can't remember anything? I don't know what happened, but you understand where I'm coming from."

"Did she have any enemies?"

"Enemies? No. She got along well with everyone. She was a special girl, believe me, Detective."

"Perhaps enemies might be too strong a word. Was there anyone she had disagreements with? Maybe over a boy?"

"Not that I'm aware."

"How about another boy or man who may have been attracted to Debbie, but she didn't return the interest?"

"She was a pretty, vibrant girl. There were plenty of boys interested in her. But I can't say there was anyone calling or harassing her in any way that I knew about."

"But there were other boys that might have been jealous of her relationship with Mr. Wheeler?"

"I'm sure there were, but why attack my Debbie? Why not Wheeler?"

"Maybe she said something that set them off. You know how kids are. Maybe she said something that she thought was harmless, but some kid took it the wrong way."

"You seem to think it was another boy and not John Wheeler."

"My responsibility to you and to the people of this county is to explore every possibility to the best of my ability."

She flashed a thin smile. "You're not going to show your hand, are you, Detective?"

I stood. "I wanted to tell you about the reopening of your daughter's case in person. We'll be in touch as things develop, and when there is something concrete you'll know about it immediately."

* * *

Derrick scrambled to his feet when Vargas came into our office. He swept up a handful of files and said, "You can sit here. I don't need a desk."

"It's okay, Derrick. I'm not staying. I just came down to tell Frank something."

"What's up?"

"Hector Machado. The dealer Mackay said he was working for."

"You tracked him down?"

"He's in a halfway house run by a church, out in Immokalee. Released eight months ago after eleven years for dealing. Here's his record; it's a long one."

She handed me a file. Machado's rap sheet was all about drug offenses. Where was the "three strikes you're out" policy for dealers? His mug shot was typical of men who'd served years in prison; Machado's tattoos couldn't cover his sallow look and dead eyes.

"Was there anything on the Pewter Mug?"

"Nobody in vice remembers a connection to drugs, but the guys who were on the force then are long gone. You want me to look further into it?"

I shook my head. "I didn't think there was. A reputation is a hard thing to clean up after it's been spoiled."

"That's how I feel. I'll see you later."

"Come on, Derrick, let's go see Machado."

* * *

Three of the men hanging out on the house's porch disappeared into the house as we pulled up. Criminals had a sixth sense when it came to spotting a cop.

I said, "Leave your jacket in the car."

We nodded as we made our way through the cigarette smoke into the house and were greeted with sounds from a TV. A sixtyish man in a cluttered office by the door served as the gatekeeper. The crude tattoos snaking around his neck verified he was a reformed man looking to pay it back.

He jumped to his feet. "Hiya doing, officers? Name's Jay Crowley. I'm the manager here."

"I'm Detective Luca, and this is Detective Dickson. We're looking to talk with Hector Machado."

He frowned. "Hector? Don't tell me he's in trouble."

"It's an old case, a twenty-five-year-old homicide."

"Homicide?"

"Nothing to do with Machado. He was used as an alibi."

"Phew. That's good. Hector's a personal project of mine. I think he's gonna be okay. He's out on the porch."

Crowley stuck his head out the door and yelled, "Hector, we need you inside."

Machado smelled like an ashtray and looked nothing like his mug shot. I had to agree with the manager—prison had taken the edge off Machado; he was a beaten man. He wouldn't be able to compete with today's cutthroat dealers and would be cleaning toilets to pay the rent on a trailer home.

"These detectives want a word with you. You got nothing to worry about."

I said, "We're working an old case."

Derrick said, "Ancient, twenty-five years old."

The manager said, "Use my office. I'll be outside."

My heart cranked up when Derrick shut the door to the tiny office. I said, "We're not here on anything you have to be concerned about. You tell us the truth, and we're out of here, okay?"

"What do you wanna know?"

"Twenty-five years ago, a girl was killed at Delnor-Wiggins Park."

Machado's eyes widened. "I don't know nothing about that."

Derrick said, "It's okay, man. A guy named Lew Mackay, he was at the park and used you as an alibi."

"Me? I wasn't there. Is somebody trying to frame me?"

"No. Look, we know you were dealing back then. This Mackay said he was working for you. Do you remember him?"

Derrick handed him an old driver's license photo of Mackay.

Machado squinted and studied the picture. "I can't say for sure. What was he supposed to be doing for me?"

I said, "He said he was dropping cash off at Delnor for a buy."

"Could be, the places that were used always changed, and I never had the drugs and money in the same place. You get pinched, you only lose one half of it."

"You used runners to drop the cash?"

He nodded.

"Isn't that risky? A guy could take off with the money."

"He wouldn't get far."

Derrick said, "Mackay said he met you at the Pewter Mug, and you gave him the cash there."

"I don't remember. But I used to go there. They got good prime rib."

"Yeah, I like their prime rib too. I've only been here a little while, but so far, it's the best in town."

Machado was being careful in admitting he was involved in a drug deal. We needed an ID on Mackay, and my partner was talking about meat.

I said, "Look, I know you don't trust us, but all we want to know is if you used Mackay. Take another look at the picture, okay?"

He took the picture and shook his head. "I don't think I know this guy."

"You're sure?"

"Yep."

"All right, let's get out of here."

"That was a waste of time. Here"—I tossed the keys to Derrick—"you drive."

"You think he was lying?"

"Good possibility, but it was a long time ago, and memories fade."

"I don't know how much money we're talking about, but if Machado entrusted it to Mackay, you'd think he'd know who he was. And if Mackay worked with him a couple of times, he'd remember him."

"That's what's bothering me. Mackay doesn't seem the type, and he's never been in trouble before."

"That's no guarantee, though. Money gets people to do the stupidest things."

The kid was right about that. "He did say he went to the Pewter Mug."

"It could be that Mackay knew who Machado was and knew he went there."

"Another lover of the prime rib?"

"It's awful. I went there once and hated it. I was just saying that to try to get him to open up."

This kid had promise. "You had me. I never had the prime rib, but the place was tired looking."

"There's water back there. Maybe someone will rip it down and put something nice up."

"We're going to need to find some way of vetting Mackay's alibi, or he's our number one."

"I have an idea. It may sound a little crazy, but why don't we ask Mackay if he wore a disguise when he made the runs."

It wasn't crazy; it was near brilliant, and something I should have realized. If Mackay was straight until he got mixed up with Machado to earn extra money, he would've wanted to stay under the radar. It looked like the Brainol memory supplement I was taking was useless.

"Not crazy, but a long shot. When we talk with him let's see if he can give us another name or two."

Chapter 11

Thirty-two-year-old Brian Boyle managed an insurance business housed in Vanderbilt Collections. The shopping center, which had gone up just as the market collapsed, was finally finding its legs and was nearly full.

In a white, long-sleeved shirt and blue tie, Brian was all business. He projected a serious air, probably the result of his sister's brutal murder.

Brian had sandy hair and guarded green eyes. He said, "You mind if we talk outside?"

"Not at all. I'm happy to get out of the AC. Is it me, or is it cold in here?"

He laughed. "Funny you'd say that. Everyone here makes fun of me when I complain it's too cold."

I walked through the door saying, "We have something in common."

I put on my Maui Jims and Boyle donned Ray-Bans, saying, "Sun feels good."

"I've only been down here a couple of years, and I'm loving Novembers."

Boyle nodded. "So, the case has been reopened. Why?"

"We received a call with new information."

"On who the killer is?"

"I can't say definitively, but you have a right to know that as I reviewed the case, I—I—let's just say it warranted a full going-over. Okay?"

He stopped dead and turned to me. "Then there were mistakes made."

"We've learned a lot in the twenty-five years since this occurred. We have different methods and new scientific tools."

"I didn't know what was going on back then. I trusted the police. I was just a kid. But as I got older, I thought a lot about what had happened. There were so many unanswered questions. When I was about twenty, I found out that Foster was inexperienced. It made me sick to my stomach. I was convinced the case was closed too fast. At first, I thought someone powerful, maybe a cop's kid or a politician, did it. Or maybe some psycho rich kid. I didn't know what to think. It consumed me."

"It had to be tough. I know it's small consolation, but getting justice helps with closure."

Boyle started walking. "I realized I had to find a way to move on or I'd turn into my mother. She stopped living when Debbie died."

I saw a bench offering shade. "Let's sit down a minute."

"What do you want from me?"

"I don't want to drudge up shit you put to bed, Brian. But I promise I'll follow any lead I find, no matter where it takes us."

"I knew it. There was a cover-up."

"No, no. There is zero evidence of anything like that. I'm just saying nothing will stop me. Okay?"

He nodded.

"There are a couple of things that are unclear to me. Clem Walker, the guy fishing on the beach, how did you run into him?"

"When John Wheeler went looking for Debbie, I stayed behind, like he said, and waited for him and my sister to come back. After a while, I started getting nervous being alone and guess I panicked. I thought maybe they had been taking a walk, you know, the romance thing. When I started looking on my own, that's when I saw Clem Walker."

"Was he nearby?"

"Yes."

"Do you think he was really fishing or maybe up to no good?"

"What do you mean? You think he was involved?"

"Like I said, I am looking at everything and everyone."

"I don't know. I never really thought about him."

"Did Walker have a bucket he was using when fishing?"

"I don't think so."

"Pretty unusual, wouldn't you say?"

"I never thought about that."

"When your sister's boyfriend came back and met up with you and Walker, what was your impression? Did he seem like someone who'd been attacked?"

He shrugged. "To be honest, I was just worried about my sister, where she was, and if she was okay."

"Was Wheeler agitated, injured?"

"He was talking fast. I couldn't catch what he was saying, and then we began searching for Debbie."

"When you started looking for your sister, did you have any sense that you were being steered where to look? Like some areas might be off-limits?"

He shrugged. "I just remember feeling helpless. I wanted my mother and kept saying we need the police."

"You asked to get the police involved?"

"Yes, I was crying. We needed help to find my sister."

"Interesting."

"What does that mean?"

"Both Wheeler and Walker claim to have been the one to insist they get the police involved."

"I was crying for help. Maybe they weren't listening because I was just a little kid."

"When you left to get help. What did you do?"

"They finally agreed to get help, and we went to John Wheeler's car."

"Did you go back to the blanket and get your things?"

"No, we just ran out of the park."

"You don't recall Wheeler going back for his shoes?"

He wagged his head. "Things were stressed. It was surreal. I can't be absolutely sure, but I don't remember going back. All I remember was running to the car."

Chapter 12

Derrick asked, "Who we going to see, Frank?"

"Igor Papadakis."

"That's the guy who said he was also walking the beach that night."

"Yep. But he didn't live anywhere near Wiggins at the time."

"Where does he live now?"

"In Estero."

Igor Papadakis lived on a sidewalk-less street off Corkscrew Road. The lime-green, cinder block home couldn't be worth more than two hundred thousand. A brown dog, chained to a stake next to a detached garage, barked as we pulled in the driveway.

Wearing a gray, button-down shirt and chinos, fifty-seven-year-old Papadakis looked ready to go out. He was caught off guard by our appearance and stumbled over his words. His teeth said American, but his accent was more Russian than Greek. Papadakis had been here for thirty years and still had a heavy accent?

The hair he had left was died jet-black, like his pencil-thin mustache. The house was dark enough to develop film in. I could smell his fear as we walked into a kitchen whose blinds were shut tight. Sitting on the counter was a copy of yesterday's *Naples Daily News* with its front-page feature touting the reopening of the Boyle case.

"Can I get you anything to drink?"

We both declined, and I said, "The Deborah Boyle case has been reopened."

He tried faking a look of puzzlement. "Oh, yes, the Wiggins-Pass girl."

"What were you doing at the park that night?"

"I went for a walk. Got to stay in shape." He patted his midsection.

"Why Wiggins?"

"It's a nice beach."

Not better than Vanderbilt, in my opinion. "But you were living in Golden Gate. You had to drive past miles of beaches to get to Wiggins."

"There's a good amount of parking at Wiggins."

"At night the parking is free by the downtown beaches. And they're close to where you lived."

"I don't like the beaches there. They're too narrow."

"Why not Lowdermilk then or Clam Pass?"

He shrugged.

Derrick said, "The beaches in Greece, they don't have sand. They're rocky, right?"

"Most are, but you can find sandy beaches if you know where to go."

This kid better learn to keep his mouth shut, and if he opens it, to ask pertinent questions, not crap a tourist would talk about.

"Where were you born?"

"St. Petersburg, Russia, but it was a difficult time with the Soviet Union collapsing, so my father moved the family to Greece. It's a beautiful country. You should go. I really miss it."

"Why did you come to America, then?"

"There were some difficulties. Greece is wonderful, but the legal, uh, the political situation is not good."

"What do you mean by that?"

"Nothing really. Just that, nice as it is, it can be frustrating there."

I said, "I still don't understand why someone would drive all the way to Wiggins, bypassing a bunch of great beaches to go to Wiggins."

"Some people like blue and others red."

"When you left Greece, you came straight to the States?"

"Yes. Athens to Miami. I stayed in Miami for a short time. I didn't like it."

"You came alone?"

"Yes, my family stayed in Greece."

"Ever been back?"

"No, maybe one day."

I couldn't take much more. "Your statement said that you never saw Debbie Boyle, her brother, or her boyfriend the night she was murdered."

"That's right. I was walking, and I think they were supposed to have been north of where I was walking."

"But your statement said when you arrived at Wiggins you parked in lot three, correct?"

"Yeah, I think that was it. It's been so long, I can't remember much."

"Let me refresh your memory, then." I opened my Moleskine and sketched a quick map. "You parked here, and this is where the Boyle party was that night. You had to walk right in front of them. Are you sure you didn't see them or hear them?"

"I was walking by the water, and when I walk I look down, like a lot of people. I didn't see them, and maybe I didn't hear anything because it was windy, and there were waves, not big ones, but still, they make sounds."

"Why didn't you come forward immediately when you heard that Debbie Boyle was murdered?"

"I didn't know anything about it."

"But you had to know someone would identify you as being there, and that was why you came forward three days later."

"No, no. I didn't think I knew anything about it, but I saw on TV they were asking for anyone who was there to come forward, and I did."

This guy was greasy, but we had nothing on him. I decided to wrap it up, and if something came up, revisit him.

Tough as it was, I kept my tongue in my mouth as we drove away from the Papadakis house.

"You okay, Frank?"

"Yeah, but in case you didn't know, that was a homicide interview, not a travel podcast."

"Sorry, I was just trying to follow up on a hunch. Just forget it. I won't let it happen again."

"Pull over."

"What?"

"Pull over, into the CVS lot."

Derrick maneuvered into a space, and I said, "You had a hunch?"

"It was just a little something, that's all; no big deal."

"That's where you're wrong. You have a hunch, a feeling, a premonition, or some sign from God, you follow it right to the end. You hear me?" I pointed my finger in his face. "Don't let anyone convince you otherwise. You got that?"

"Yeah, sure, but take it easy."

"I don't want you to carry what I've been lugging around since I became a homicide detective. Some poor kid hung himself because I didn't have the balls to stand up for what I believed in."

"Oh my God. What happened?"

"I was a rookie, and just like you, paired with a seasoned detective. But this guy was on his way out; his retirement just a couple of months away. A girl was strangled, and this kid, Barrow, was a person of interest because she dumped him as a boyfriend. We picked him up, and though he didn't help himself in the interview, we had nothing on him. The girl who was murdered was related to a politician, and there was a lot of pressure to arrest someone. My partner wanted to arrest Barrow, but I knew we didn't have enough. To make a long story short, they began to pressure me, saying the department wouldn't look good and all that team player crap. I went against my gut and agreed. I said I'd go along to keep the peace and fit in. I didn't want to get my partner mad. It was as stupid as it gets. We arrested Barrow, and he hangs himself his first night behind bars."

"Oh my God."

"It was terrible. The father and the papers were all over us. I didn't think it could get worse, but it did."

"What happened?"

"Some felon admits he was the one who killed the girl. The Barrow kid was innocent, and I had a hand in killing him."

"I don't think you're being fair to yourself."

"What happened, happened. I've learned to live with it, but I'm telling you, when you feel something, follow it. Don't let anyone persuade you otherwise. You got that?"

"Okay. I'll keep that in mind."

"Good. Now, what was that hunch you had?"

"I could be off base, but this Papadakis, he gets out of Russia and lands in Greece. He said he loved Greece and his family is still there. But he's never been back? Does that sound right to you?"

"Sometimes life has a way of getting you on a treadmill."

"Maybe, but first, he slipped about the legal system, then he gave us that BS about the political situation."

"It's not easy to live in another country. Things don't work they like do in the States."

"He was coming from Russia, where everything was collapsing."

It was a good point. "Fair enough, but I don't get what you're thinking."

"You know what I think? I think this Papadakis got in trouble in Greece and had to take off. Maybe there's another dead girl somewhere because of him."

A multicontinental serial killer? Baseless speculation, but I couldn't totally blow it off, not after the serial killing last year, which almost cost me my career. "Interesting, but he hasn't done anything in the last twenty-five years."

"That we know about."

"Maybe. What would your action plan look like?"

"Hunt around some, ask Interpol, the Greeks, and see what comes up on Papadakis."

"Okay, but I don't have a lot of time to put into it at this point."

Chapter 13

I read over the autopsy report again. Debbie Boyle had been stabbed four times in the face, once in her chest, and six in her midsection. There seemed to be no doubt the killer was angry. She had several superficial slashes that I believed came when she struggled to fight off her attacker.

Boyle was athletic; she would have put up a fight, even if surprised by her killer. None of the wounds individually were deadly. So, even if she knew her killer, she would have attempted to fight him or her off.

"Derrick, come here."

"Yes, sir."

I pointed to the autopsy report. "The victim suffered several deep wounds, but she also had superficial wounds on her arms and right shoulder. What does that tell you?"

"She was trying to get away."

"That's good. I'd like you to check with all the hospitals in the area, including Lee County, and see if anyone showed up in their emergency room that night or the next morning with any knife wounds."

"Man, that's a great idea."

The kid was growing on me.

I got back to the autopsy report. The face wounds were bothering me; someone was either really pissed at her or was deranged. Assuming it was anger, it could be another woman looking to destroy her looks. There was the blond woman that Mrs. Nielsen mentioned, or it could be a lover she dumped.

We needed more background on her love life. Time to visit more of her friends and family. I would love to avoid seeing the mother again. Her pain was still heartbreakingly evident after all these years. What kind of kid was Debbie? I needed the truth, not Mommy's impression. Were there any drugs or drinking?

I pulled out the blood panels. The toxicology report came up empty for illicit drugs and poisons.

* * *

Joanne Wilbur had been one of three girlfriends that were close to Debbie. They all went to Barron Collier High School and were on the cheerleading team together. Wilbur was a realtor, causing me to wonder how long it'd take her to inform me she was ready to help me with my real estate needs.

We settled under an umbrella at a Starbucks close to her Pine Ridge office. She wore outsized sunglasses and too much lipstick. Her body language was aggressive, but she spoke softly.

"You caught me off guard with the news about Debbie. God, it was so long ago. I'm embarrassed to say I hadn't thought about her in a long while."

"Life has a way of moving on."

"So true. I'd been so upset about her for so long." She shook her head. "It was shocking what happened, and to have someone get away with it? It sucked the life out of all of us, especially her poor mother."

"How long did you know her?"

She laughed. "We'd been friends since we could walk, maybe even before that. Our mothers brought us to the first Gymboree place down here, and that's where we met."

"Friends drift in and out of each other's lives at times. Was that how it was with you and Debbie?"

"No, not really. We went to the same schools, and sometimes if we had different schedules we'd make other friends, but we were always close."

"What did you think of John Wheeler?"

"John? You think it really was him?"

People like to talk, so I said, "I can't discuss the case, but I can say that there is nothing that would make Mr. Wheeler a stronger suspect than many others."

She looked over her sunglasses at me. "I don't know what that means, but I'll leave it there."

"Thanks. Now, about Mr. Wheeler?"

"He was nice. I mean, it was pretty exciting to have a guy with a car at the time. She started with him before she got her license. We had some good times together."

"He was quite a bit older than Debbie. Did she like older guys?"

"Yeah, but we all did. You know, the guys in our classes were kinda geeky or into sports, and the older guys were working or in college."

"Did Debbie have other boyfriends?"

"Sure. She was good at getting what she wanted. I guess you could call her a flirt."

"If she was interested in a man, she'd make it known?"

"Maybe not so, uh, overtly, but yeah, he'd get the message."

"Was she sexually active?"

Wilbur's cheeks reddened. "I guess so."

"You guess so, or you know so?"

"She'd tell me things. I mean, she was no runaround or anything like that. But I know there were at least two."

"Did she have any enemies? Anyone who would wish her harm?"

She shook her head. "Not to do anything like that."

"Her mother said everyone loved Debbie. Is that true?"

"Of course she'd say that. What mother wouldn't?"

I could think of a long list of mothers who knew their kids were terrors. "Are you saying there were some that didn't like her?"

"She was a pretty popular girl, and you know how kids can be. At times, she could be a little nasty, but who isn't?"

"Did she ever tell you if anyone got physical with her?"

"You mean like hit her?"

I nodded.

"She would've told me. But she'd never stand for that; she'd fight back. She took jujitsu and gymnastics. Debbie was strong for a girl. But she'd never start anything. I mean, she wouldn't even step on a bug. We used to make fun of her. If there was a bug in the house she would shoo it outside."

"Was she the kind who would fight back if attacked?"

"No doubt in my mind. She never seemed scared. I know she faked it plenty of times, but Debbie wouldn't back down; it wasn't in her DNA."

"Was there anyone she flirted with but never followed through with? Someone who may have expected something to happen and it didn't?"

"I don't know. I mean, we all would lead guys on a bit. Not all the time, but it was a little game, you know?"

I did know. Except it was no game chasing down guys who'd end up raping a girl who had gone too far.

"Any particular situations that might have gone too far?"

She frowned. "There was this kid, Jason Norwicky. At the end of our sophomore year, Debbie was teasing him. I think she really liked him, but maybe because he was our age or something, they never hooked up. One time, at lunch, she was laying it on pretty heavy, you know, whispering in his ear and leaning against him. When we went out to the yard he pinned her against the building and she started screaming. The teachers went nuts, and he got suspended for a week."

"What happened after that?"

"There was bad blood. I knew Debbie felt bad about it. Most of the school knew she flirted with him, but she put up a total front about it, denying she led him on, and eventually it died down."

"Any other similar incidents?"

"I don't like bringing all this dirt up. The poor girl is dead. She wasn't perfect, but she certainly didn't deserve what happened to her."

I pressed her for more names, got two, and left to see another close friend of the victim.

Chapter 14

It was Mary Ann's birthday, and there was no better place to celebrate than Bleu Provence. The weather was so nice there was no way you could sit indoors. The patio was bustling, but the lighting and the vegetation kept it romantic.

They had the best wine list in town. The hundred-page list would normally intimidate me, but there were Jacque's selections—a clever listing of the owner's reasonably priced favorites. Grabbing the list, I thumbed through, in case anyone was watching, before choosing a Rhone Valley Grenache off the suggested list.

We'd been going out for a year, an event we celebrated with a catamaran cruise at sunset, and it felt good. I'd moved out of the cabana and into Mary Ann's bedroom. It was my only serious relationship since my divorce. We had been partners for about two years, and the thought to date her never crossed my mind until I got bladder cancer. I still don't know if it was the way she helped me deal with it or if it was the cancer that changed me. Either way, I was happier than I'd been in years.

Women approaching forty rarely like to make a big deal about their birthday, so clinking glasses, I said *"centi'anni,"* wishing us both a hundred more years, in Italian. I didn't know what smelled better, her peachy perfume or the wine's licorice aroma.

Mary Ann wore a simple black dress, caressing her in all the right places, with the earrings I bought her for our anniversary. I nudged my chair closer and kissed her shoulder.

"This is perfect. We gotta find a way to freeze time."

"If only we could. But the next best thing is to be present in the moment, Frank."

"I am."

She raised her eyebrows. "Really?"

"Well, I'm trying. Give me that, okay?"

She weaved her fingers through mine. "That's all we can do; try our hardest, and miracles happen."

The word miracle distracted me. I started thinking of a baby and the fact both of us would probably never be parents. Mary Ann had never talked about it, though I knew she loved kids. I wanted to know what she really felt about it, but having a discussion like that scared me.

"Frank?"

"Oh, sorry, I was just thinking I have to do better, like you said."

She smiled and picked up the menu. "What are you thinking of having?"

"Probably the Loup de mer."

"You always get that."

I put my hand on her thigh. "When I like something, I stick with it."

After we ordered, Mary Ann said, "We should take a trip to France. Go to Paris and maybe the south of France. It's supposed to be gorgeous there."

"That'd be nice. If the food's anything close to this, I'm in."

"Maybe we could spend a couple of days in Paris, see the Eiffel Tower and the Louvre. It's right up there with the Uffizi in Florence."

Museums? Ugh, I liked art as much as the next guy but couldn't spend hours in a museum. I hoped Mary Ann looked at art like she shopped. Go in, see what you wanted to see, and get out.

"The Louvre is where the *Mona Lisa* is, right?"

"Yeah, it's a lot smaller than you'd expect. Plus, I read you can't get close to it after that lunatic tried to destroy it."

It was mildly comforting to know there were sick bastards all over the globe.

"I like the impressionist painters like Monet and Renoir."

"Impressionist? You always surprise me, Frank."

A waiter brought our food, and we continued to chat about taking a trip.

Washing a piece of smoked salmon down with wine, I caught a glimpse through the patio windows of a woman with blond hair. I finished my appetizer and was refilling my glass when the base of my skull vibrated.

Mary Ann said, "Since it's our first time, we should probably go for about ten days total. You lose at least a full day traveling, and we could spend four days in Paris and—"

The woman was pregnant.

"You think Debbie Boyle could have been pregnant?"

"What?"

"If Debbie Boyle was pregnant, that could be what motivated someone to kill her. It could have been Wheeler looking to end the pregnancy."

"We're not going to be talking about this, but she could have gotten an abortion."

"Maybe she didn't want to. Maybe she wanted to keep the baby."

"Maybe you ought to try harder at being present, Frank."

She pushed her chair back.

"Where are you going?"

"To the ladies' room."

* * *

Derrick set a coffee down on my desk. I tipped the cover open—chocolate brown. "Thanks. Last night I thought of something."

"The Boyle case?"

I nodded. "What if Debbie Boyle was pregnant? That would provide Wheeler with motive."

"Interesting angle."

"Or it could be a girl or woman whose boyfriend impregnated Boyle. She went bonkers and killed her. It would explain the facial wounds."

"Why wouldn't they have checked during the autopsy?"

"It's not standard procedure."

"No way to know now."

"Depends how far along she was. We need to find out how sexually active she was. Boyle was only seventeen, but that doesn't mean anything."

"You're telling me. In DC we'd see pregnant girls as young as twelve all the time."

I hesitated before saying, "Call the woman I went to see: Joanne Wilbur. Here's her card. But you gotta be careful; this is delicate stuff, okay?"

"Of course. I understand."

"I'm going to see another close friend of the victim, a woman named Janet Lipton."

* * *

Pelican Landing was a massive community in Bonita Springs on the west side of Route 41. It was spread over twenty-five-hundred acres, bordered by Spring Creek and Estero Bay, where it had its own beach club.

Lipton lived in a subcommunity called Astor. A two-car garage door dominated the view of the blue home from the curb, overpowering the multicolored paver driveway. A pair of brown wooden entry doors were framed by royal palm trees.

I pressed the bell as a stainless steel wind chime tinkled, making me wonder who really liked the sound it made.

Janet Lipton's worn-out look was countered by the sparkle in her eyes and her warm handshake.

"Nice to meet you, Detective. Come in. You know, you look just like George Clooney."

It was the first time in a while I had gotten the Clooney reference, and it felt good. "Really? I'll take that as a compliment; though I don't like his politics."

A pile of backpacks under a foyer table covered with photos of kids explained the tired look.

"It's a beautiful day; we should talk out on the lanai."

"Sounds good."

We walked through a family room that had cathedral ceilings and onto a small covered lanai. There was a cage over the pool and a slice of a lake view.

"Why don't you tell me about Debbie, how long you knew her, and what was she like?"

"Well, we'd been friends since the fourth grade. We were in Mrs. Macaster's class, and we sat next to each other. Nancy was in the same class. I was drawn to her, I guess. She was, I don't know, fearless? She was always the first to try something. She'd raise her hand whether she knew the answer or not, but most of all she was just fun."

"Popular?"

"For sure. She was always part of the 'in' group."

"Could she be mean?"

"Mean? No, I wouldn't say she was mean, but she could be stubborn."

"What do you mean by stubborn?"

"When she wanted to do something, you couldn't tell her no, even if it was something dangerous."

"Can you give me an example?"

"There were these boys; they were much older, in college, who we met at a high school football game. Debbie had just quit cheerleading; she said it was stupid. So, we were hanging out with them a little, but I got a bad feeling about them because they kept whispering to each other and laughing. Debbie was bored with the game and wanted to leave. The boys asked if we wanted to go for a ride down to Clam Pass. I said no because we didn't know them, but Debbie hopped in the car with them."

"Did anything happen?"

"No. But my point was you don't get in cars with strange boys; she knew it was wrong but did it anyway."

"Tell me about her relationship with John Wheeler."

"They were hot and heavy for a while. She had her eye on him since we were freshmen. Like I said, she got what she wanted."

"After she got what she wanted, did she move on? Grow bored?"

"Depends. She was loyal, but at times, I don't know. Let's just say Debbie was a little contradictory, but who isn't?"

I got it the kid was human, but I knew she was holding back. "Now you have me confused. Can you explain?"

"Sorry. Debbie wanted to do the right thing all the time. She worked with the disadvantaged kids from Immokalee through the church, but then she'd be saying how good-looking Father Harrigan was and whether he was celibate or not. For a time, I thought there was something going on between them."

"Why was that?"

"She was spending more time with him, and the way they looked at each other, it made me suspicious."

"Did she ever say anything about it?"

"She'd laugh at me, one minute denying it and then giving the impression something was going on the next minute."

"She liked to keep people off balance?"

She nodded. "That's a good way of putting it. I hope I didn't give you the impression she was a runaround. I mean, she was no nun, but she wasn't, you know . . ."

"Got it. Joanne Wilbur told me a story about some kid, Norwicky, that Debbie led on and which he read as her being interested in him."

"Well, she did lead him on, as far as I was concerned, but he still shouldn't have imposed himself on her."

"She said he was suspended from school."

"Yeah, and it wasn't the first time she accomplished that."

"There was another one?"

"Yeah, but it was an entirely different situation. We had to take the SAT tests, and we did okay on them, but this kid Gerry, he got sky-high scores, even though he wasn't the greatest student. There was a rumor that he had gotten a copy of the test in advance and had cheated. Gerry was interested in Debbie, but she didn't want anything to do with him. Well, Debbie goes and starts saying that Gerry had offered her the test in advance, but she turned him down. She had no proof, and everybody started to call her a liar. Then, out of nowhere, she said she had gone to Mr. Culver before the test and told him. It didn't make sense. Mr. Culver, we used to call him Mr. C, was a real handsome, younger teacher. Why would she go to him and not the principal or guidance counselor?"

"What happened?"

"The school got wind of it and brought Debbie in. All of sudden, there's Mr. C saying that she had gone to him about Gerry stealing the test, but he said there was no proof at the time and he didn't report it."

"Gerry, what's his last name? He must have been pretty upset."

"Moore, Gerry Moore. They made him take the test over by himself, and he didn't do as well."

"So, Debbie was telling the truth?"

"She'd never say, but it was a really weird situation."

"Was this Gerry Moore the type of guy who'd seek to even the score?"

"He was mad, no doubt, and he said he'd get even."

"You heard him say that?"

She nodded. "He said, 'You wait, you bitch. I'll get you. You're gonna pay for this.'"

Chapter 15

"Boss, I was thinking a lot about this case, and it hit me, maybe we should be looking for older men who liked younger girls. You can't trust those sleazebags; they're perverted. I tried checking the databases they had back then; they're nothing like the sex-offenders registry we have now. So, I checked arrests for sex offenses two years before the killing."

The kid's resourcefulness was impressive. "Anyone interesting?"

"There were three sleazebags, but two of them were in jail at the time."

"Get to it, Derrick."

"Matt Boralis. He was arrested about two months before for attempting to lure a fifteen-year-old into his car. Guess where it took place."

"Delnor-Wiggins."

"Yep, and it wasn't his first time. The creep posed as a photographer. Said he was going to take pictures of the girl and get her a chance at modeling."

"Did the creep do any time?"

"Got off both times. But here's the interesting thing; I don't know for sure, but I ran Boralis through the national system. A Mary Boralis came up, could be a sister or a relative of some sort. She was a sixteen-year-old who was sexually assaulted and stabbed to death."

"When was that?"

"Nineteen eighty-four."

"Good work, Derrick. Let's go see this bag of shit."

* * *

Matt Boralis looked like a cross between John Goodman and Jackie Gleason. A young girl's desire to be a model was a lot stronger than I imagined. Otherwise, Boralis would need a gun, not a camera, to get a girl to follow him.

Boralis stepped outside, jowls shaking as he spoke. The sun glinted off his black, plaster-like hair. He kept his hand on the doorknob, his yellow shirt revealing a crater-sized belly button.

"We have some questions for you, Mr. Boralis. It'd be better if we did this inside."

"Uh, no, out here's okay."

Was he hiding something? "That's up to you." I dug out my cell. "I gotta get this, but don't wait for me, you can start, Derrick."

I jogged to the Cherokee, jumped in the driver's seat, put the cell to my ear, and threw the strobe lights on. Seconds later, I had to stifle a laugh when Boralis waved a tree-limb sized arm and opened the door for us.

Boralis went in first, picking up a couple of magazines that look like porn to me. The place was dark and ice cold. I buttoned my jacket, and we followed him into the kitchen. I felt like we stepped into the 1950s: Formica countertops, a black-and-white tiled floor, and a lime-green refrigerator.

Derrick elbowed me, throwing a chin toward a picture of a carhop on roller skates. She was bent over a car with no underpants. How can you have something like that in the kitchen? A basement or bar area, maybe, but not a kitchen.

We settled into chairs with chrome legs, and I said, "Did you know Debbie Boyle?"

"No. Why would you think I would?"

"Because she looked like the type of girl you'd try to lure into taking a ride with you."

"That's ridiculous."

"Is it? You were arrested at Delnor-Wiggins for attempting to lure a similar girl, and you call it a ridiculous assumption?"

Boralis pulled a handkerchief out and dabbed his forehead. "You have it wrong. The girl saw my camera and asked me what kind of photographer I was. I told her my area of focus was the modeling industry. She asked me about my connections and wanted her pictures taken. That's all it was."

"You presented yourself as a model photographer, correct?"

"Not a professional one, but yes, I've taken pictures of women before."

"And you don't take pictures, say, of landscapes or things like that?"

"No. It's the human element I find fascinating."

"And were you alone that day at Wiggins?"

"Yes."

"So, why bring your camera if not to use as a prop to fool some poor girl into thinking you were a model photographer?"

"I did nothing wrong. The charges were dropped."

Derrick said, "You have any pictures of Mary Boralis?"

"She was my sister. Of course I have pictures of her."

I said, "I'll bet she had blond hair, didn't she?"

"Why are you so interested in my sister? She's been dead a long time."

"She was sexually assaulted and stabbed to death."

"It was a very sad day."

"Did you have anything to do with her death?"

"Now who's being ridiculous, Detective? That was my little sister, who I miss every day of my life."

"Did you take pictures of her too?"

"I resent your tone, Detective. I haven't done anything wrong and have tried to cooperate with you, but I must ask you to leave."

We didn't have grounds to stay, so we left.

"What did you think, boss?"

"He's a creep, but unless we can put him at the scene that night, we have nothing."

"You want me to find a picture of what he looked like back then and see if anybody can identify him?"

It was a long shot on top of a long shot but a damn good idea. "Knock yourself out."

Chapter 16

"Frank, I wasn't able to—"

I held a hand and reached for the case file. "Derrick, do you remember anything in the Boyle case file about a Gerry Moore?"

"Moore? No, I don't think so. What's going on?"

"It could be nothing, but about a year before Boyle was murdered, this kid Moore threatened her."

"Over what?"

"Boyle made an allegation that Moore stole a copy of the SAT test beforehand."

"Where would he get access to a copy?"

"I don't know. There was no proof he stole it. It came down to her word against his, until a teacher came forward and said Boyle had told him about it."

"Why didn't the teacher do anything about it?"

"Since there was no evidence, he probably didn't want to mess up Moore's reputation."

"If Moore threatened her, we have to look into him."

I closed the file. "No doubt. It doesn't look like anyone talked with Moore, at least formally. We'll fix that. What did you want to say before?"

"No hospital in the area has any record of anyone coming into the emergency room the night of or the day after Debbie Boyle's body was found."

"It doesn't surprise me."

"I really thought we'd come up with something."

"It was a long shot, but you had a good idea, kid."

"Thanks. Frank, we're supposed to be partners, right?"

"Not supposed to be, we are."

"Can I ask you something, and you won't get mad?"

I didn't like his setup. "Sure. Ask away."

"Can you stop calling me kid? I'm not a kid. I know you're more experienced than I am, but when you call me kid, especially in front of others, it makes me seem like I'm some kind of an intern."

The kid was green but right. I stood and stuck my hand out. "Sorry, partner, I didn't realize it bothered you. Telling me was the right thing to do. If we're going to be partners, we gotta be straight with each other."

Derrick smiled like a kid at a pet shop. "Thanks, Frank."

"Can you do me a favor and find out where this Gerry Moore is living? I'm going to go see Campo, the guy who found Boyle's body."

Derrick's smile crumpled. "Uh, sure. I think I'm qualified enough to do that."

Uh-oh. "Going to see Campo is probably a waste of time, but you're welcome to take the ride."

"Nah, it's okay."

"You sure? I don't feel like driving."

Derrick walked away. "Now you think I'm a caddy or something?"

Who said men let shit roll off their backs? This kid was moodier than a woman with her period. "Hold on now. I've got a lot of homicide experience. It doesn't mean I know everything, but I know properly allocating the resources we have is critical to rack up solves. We don't need to double-team a minor player. You want to come for the experience? That's fine with me."

"I think it's important to see how you do it, Frank."

I tossed him the keys to the Cherokee. "Let's get rolling."

* * *

Naples RV Resort was an RV park off Collier Boulevard that was used primarily by vacationers. Bert Campo was one of a handful of full-timers who called it home. A tiny space marked 247 was the plot where Campo was hooked up. His RV was nothing more than a pickup truck with an aluminum room bolted on.

The white vehicle had an orange strip around its midsection and was rusting in several spots. Halfway up the gravel walkway I smelled marijuana. Before I could say anything, Derrick said, "Smells like weed."

I nodded. "This should be interesting."

The sound of Pink Floyd's *The Dark Side of the Moon* bled through the trailer's louvered windows. When Campo answered the door, it all came together—Bert Campo looked like Jerry Garcia from the Grateful Dead.

"Hey, there. Come on in."

Derrick took a step and I grabbed his elbow. "If you don't mind, I'm claustrophobic, and the three us"—I pointed inside and shook my head—"it may not work for me."

"Hey, man, whatever works for you, no problemo. We can sit around back."

Around back? We followed Campo behind his trailer, where a picnic table sat on a piece of artificial grass. It was an odd setup but was shaded by a willow tree. We took seats opposite Campo, who said, "Oh, man, I forgot to ask, you want something to drink or anything?"

Not in the mood for Mountain Dew or granola, I said, "No thanks. How's your memory?"

"Memory? Uh, what's that?" He laughed and tugged on his bushy beard.

Derrick giggled. "That was good."

"I like to toke every now and then, but it don't affect my memory."

Every now and then? The tips of his forefinger and thumb were stained brown. "You were at Delnor-Wiggins Park the night Debbie Boyle was murdered."

"Yeah, it was a bummer, man."

"Tell us how you discovered her body."

"Well, I used to stay at a lot of places before I settled in here. You used to be able to stay in a bunch of places and nobody would chase you out. But now? Forget it, man. It's not worth the hassle, that's why I settled here."

Derrick said, "Please tell us about the body."

"Oh yeah. So, that night, I remember, it was a real nice night, and you know, I partied a little and must've nodded out. It was a super night, and when I woke up I had to take a leak real bad. The bathroom, the one by, I think it's parking area two or something, was always open. The lock was broken for ages, man. They never fixed it. I don't know why—"

I said, "Mr. Campo, please get back to finding the body."

"Sure, sure, no problem. So, like I was saying, I had to go pee, and I headed to the bathroom. You know, my RV don't fit real well in the regular parking lot, so I was kinda parking, you know, like, long ways—"

I wanted to strangle this guy, but Derrick said, "Please, the body."

"Yeah, I was walking to the bathroom building. I cut through, otherwise I'd have to take the path all the way around. Sometimes I do that, but I had to go bad. So, I'm coming up a hill, not a hill but like a mound, and I thought my eyes were tricking me. It looked like a body laying there. At first, I figured they was sleeping in the park, camping out like me, but without an RV. But then, I was looking, and there was no sleeping bag or nothing. No things you need when you camp out, and I slowed up and took a couple of steps toward the body, and that's when I saw her. I called out a couple of times, but she never moved."

"What did you do next?"

"It sounds crazy, man, but I had to go, so I went by the mangroves and drained the lizard."

"After you relieved yourself, what did you do?"

"All the time I'm pissing, I'm thinking of what to do. It was a total downer. I had a good head, but man, it came crashing down when I saw that poor girl."

"Did you touch the body?"

"Yeah, I went over, all the time I was like saying, 'Hey, you okay? You need help?'"

"I assume she didn't respond."

He shook his head. "No, man. When I got closer, I knelt down and saw her face. Oh man, I almost puked. How can someone do something so violent to another human being? I mean, we share the planet. We're in this life together."

"You said you touched the body. How so?"

"Nothing big, she was laying kind of on her side. So, I grabbed her shoulder, to shake it, and then I saw the blood. Man, it was a total drag."

"What next?"

"I stood up and looked around. For a second, I was afraid, really scared. Whoever did this could be out there, so I checked around. Then, I headed to the beach."

"The beach?"

"Yeah, she needed help. I didn't know what to do."

"Why not call for help?"

"I didn't have a phone. That was way before cell phones, and a lot of times people are walking the beach. I thought I could find someone and figure out what to do."

"Did you see anyone?"

"No. So, I knew I had to get in my RV and find a phone or a cop."

"And did you leave the park?"

"I was going to, but I saw cop car lights, and I just waited for the cops to come."

I pointed. "You had this RV with you that night?"

"Yeah, I've had her forever. She was a lot younger back then."

"You said you were going to the bathroom when you found the body, right?"

"Yeah, that was what I was doing, nothing else, just taking a—"

"And you said you had to go really bad."

"Yep, that's right."

"Why would you leave your RV when you had a bathroom right there and go to one at the park?"

He smiled. "I don't have much money, never did, never will. Money's not important to me, but I still got to stretch it out the best I can. I didn't like paying to dump my waste. Rather use the public facility when I can."

Derrick said, "Did you hear anything unusual that night?"

"No, nothing like a scream or anything like that."

"Did you see anyone acting suspiciously or doing anything unusual?"

"Like I said, it was a really sweet night, and there were other people there, you know, walking the beach and fishing. There was a man, I wouldn't say he was suspicious or anything, but he was hanging around the parking lot area. He could've been waiting on a ride. That's what I thought at the time."

"Where did he go?"

"I don't know, last I saw him he was hanging around the parking lot. Maybe his ride came and got him."

Derrick asked, "When the victim, Debbie Boyle, went missing, her boyfriend said he went looking for her. Did you see anyone searching the area?"

"No, but I was inside the RV."

"He claimed to be calling out her name as he tried to find her. You didn't hear anything?"

He shook his head. "Can't say I did."

I said, "It was a nice night; you probably had your windows open, and you heard nothing?"

"I didn't. If I did, I would say it. I got nothing to hide."

"You were stoned and zonked out, weren't you?"

Campo smiled. "I sleep like a baby, always have."

I stood. "That's all for now, Mr. Campo."

Derrick handed him a card. "If you remember anything else, please give us a call. We could use the help on this one."

Chatting with this pothead could have been a total waste of time, but I was hoping the next time Derrick challenged the way I prioritized, the way I used my resources, he'd think twice.

Chapter 17

The security office of Waterside Shops was smaller than the cells we stuck the bad guys in. Thankfully, it was another brilliant day. November had been flawless, and December was off to an amazing start. I left Derrick watching the monitors and had parked my ass on a bench surrounded by water features.

Only because it was December was I able to tolerate the holiday music and Santa outfits. A steady stream of shoppers moved from store to store, buying their Christmas gifts, reminding me I had to find something for Mary Ann.

I'd learned my lesson not to take the easy way out with a gift certificate, like I did for her birthday. What could I get her that would surprise her and put me in good stead? I scanned the storefronts. The place was ground zero for expensive retailers.

The front doors of Louis Vuitton were swinging open more often than a McDonald's. She'd be shocked if I ever put one of their bags under the tree. Mary Ann said the prices they get for those bags wasn't worth it, but I wonder if she really wanted one. I could swing it if I had to, but I'd rather spend the money on something else, like the trip to Europe she really wanted.

Maybe I should do some checking, get some numbers together for a trip to Paris and Rome. I could put pictures of the Colosseum and the Eiffel Tower in a card and hide the card in a big box. She'd never guess.

How much would that trip cost? There were cheap airfares in the paper all the time. I had to be careful not to get stuck like a sardine, risking a claustrophobic attack. I took my phone out to get an idea on air fares when Derrick called. The bag ring had walked into the handbag department.

I was closer to Saks than the security office. I slung my jacket over a shoulder, ripped off my tie, and sauntered into the department store. Making a left into the men's shoe department, I examined a five-hundred-dollar sneaker by Ferragamo as the final pair of crooks entered. Each couple was holding hands and kept their sunglasses on. As they headed to the Prada display, I made eye contact with one of our crew and stepped up to a sport jacket display near the exit.

Holding up a gray jacket, I spotted the leader. A twenty-something Hispanic dressed for a GQ magazine photo shoot. He was holding a bag against his female companion and reached for his earpiece. He slowly moved his head, like a cougar poised to attack. He put the bag down, put his arm around his girl, and headed for the doors.

We'd been made. The three other couples slowly moved out of the handbag area, faking interest in apparel items, before leaving the store. What went wrong? I headed to the security office.

* * *

"How the hell did they make us? Did you see anything, Derrick?"

"Uh, I think they saw you."

"Me? Can't be."

"Pretty sure it was, boss."

"I was way behind them, in the shoe department, no place near them."

"I think they saw something, maybe the bulge from your holster."

"Nah, can't be."

"Take a look at this."

Derrick rewound the video. "See here, that's you coming in. Now, here, see this guy in shorts?"

A gray-haired man in yellow cargo shorts and a Tommy Bahama shirt pulled open the first set of doors. He was twenty feet behind me. I never sensed him. He came through the second set of doors and made like he was reading a map of the store. He eyed me leaving the shoe department, and as soon as I lifted the sport jacket he turned around and left the store.

Then he took two steps and reached into his pants pocket. Derrick said, "Pretty sure that's a walkie-talkie."

I collapsed into a chair.

"Don't worry, we'll get them next time."

"If there is a fucking next time."

"Nobody has to know what spooked them. We're partners; we've got to watch each other's backs."

"Thanks, but you have to understand that some lines get crossed; there's no protecting anybody. You hear me?"

* * *

We sat down for dinner on the lanai. Mary Ann had made peas and macaroni, a comfort dish that was one of my favorites. This woman had bugged me or truly had a sixth sense. I wanted to ask her what time today she decided to make it.

Mary Ann spooned out my dish. "What's wrong, Frank?"

"Nothing."

"Don't tell me nothing. You haven't said a word since you got home."

"Not the best of days, that's all."

"Bored with the surveillance?"

Spreading cheese on my pasta, I said, "I wish."

"What happened?"

"We got made, and I was the one who blew it."

I told her what had happened, and she said, "It's no big deal. You had no idea how many lookouts they were using."

"That's bullshit. You're too good a cop to say something like that. I should have been more careful. It was a rookie mistake. If Derrick made it, I would have run it up his ass."

"You're human, Frank."

"It was reckless of me. We've been running this operation for weeks, and I pissed it down the drain."

"Nobody got hurt, and besides, you don't know for sure it was you who triggered them to run. Who knows? Maybe they made one of our dummy sales girls."

She was trying to cheer me up, and it wasn't working. My desire to be in the middle of the action had gotten to me. Some mentor I'm turning out to be.

"Let's drop it, can we?"

"How's the pasta piselli?"

"Almost as good as my mother's. You must have some Italian blood in you."

"There's a lot of Italians in Brazil. They left Italy during World War II."

I nodded. "I know. Argentina as well."

"We should go one day."

"Thought we were going to try to go to Europe?"

"You really want to go?"

I had my Christmas gift. "Sure, it's something you want to do. We should think seriously about doing it."

She put her fork down. "It can't be just about me, Frank."

"It's not. I want to go, really. It'll be great."

She grabbed my hand. "I'm so excited. I always wanted to go to Paris."

"Maybe we can do Rome as well."

"Really? Oh my God, Rome and Paris! We may never come back."

"How long a trip should we take? I don't want to be rushing around trying to get everything in."

"We could probably see most of everything in three days in each place. So, that's six days. plus two traveling days."

"And a day to get from Paris to Rome. So that's nine. We should plan minimum ten days, maybe twelve so we can do a side trip or two."

"I can get away for two weeks."

"If it's quiet, like now, no problem for me. I've got the time in the bank."

"What's going on with the Boyle case?"

"Speaking about Europe, Derrick's off on an immigrant who was at the scene. I think it's way out there, but I was going to see this kid who threatened Boyle over an SAT test. Turns out this kid moved away right after Boyle was murdered."

Chapter 18

I flew up Route 75, but traffic built steadily as I approached Sarasota. The roads were too narrow, and construction cranes dotted the skyline. It was another town whose growth outpaced its infrastructure.

The heart of Sarasota had water everywhere, but the only water on Gerry Moore's street was a rain puddle. A dog began yapping when I rang the bell. A man's voice tried to quiet the dog before he opened the door.

A barking, white ball of fur made a beeline for my leg. It was a cute dog I pegged as a Maltese.

"Sorry. Mabel, get over here."

"It's okay."

Gerry Moore scooped up the dog. His golf shirt stretched across his muscular shoulders and strained over his biceps. This guy was my age. How did he do it? Maybe Mary Ann was right, and I had to start going to the gym. If it weren't for his blond hair going pewter, he could pass for thirty.

The confirmation he was a gym rat was sealed when we shook hands. Moore wasn't earning a living doing manual labor.

"She's a Maltese, right?"

"Yeah, she's a good girl, just gets excited when anyone comes by."

As I reached out to pet the dog, she began licking my hand. She was cute. "Don't have a dog, but if I did, it'd be a Maltese."

"They've got great dispositions. Come on in."

The place looked like something you'd see in a Scandinavian movie—low-slung wooden furniture with a spartan feel. No plush sofa to kick back on; it was thin cushions all around. It felt like a classier Ikea.

A glass wall led to a patio backing up to a dense, tropical preserve. It was too rain foresty for my taste, but it seemed serene.

"Nice home, been here long?"

"Not this place, but in Sarasota about fifteen years. Let's sit here. You want something to drink?"

I settled into a low chair with a curved back. "Water, if you don't mind."

Moore opened the refrigerator and said, "I still don't understand what you wanted to talk about."

As he handed me a bottle of Fuji water, I said, "I'm working a cold case from twenty-five years ago. We were both teenagers then." I twisted the cap and took a sip. "A girl you went to school with then was murdered in Naples."

Moore turned so pale he looked like an outline in a coloring book. "Oh, an old murder."

A flag. He didn't mention Boyle. How many girls did he know who had been murdered when he was seventeen?

"You don't remember the murder of Debbie Boyle?"

He was pressing his palm on the bottle's cap. "Sure. That was a long time ago."

"I understand you had a run-in with her. She claimed you had stolen the SAT exam."

"She made the whole thing up. I don't like to talk bad since she's gone, but Debbie was a bitch. I never liked her. She came on to me a couple of times, and I had zero interest in her. She didn't like it and made up the story about the test."

"You spurned Debbie Boyle's advances, and she fabricates the SAT test theft as a way to get back at you?"

"Why else would she do something like that?"

"I hear you got in a lot of trouble with the school."

"They wanted to suspend me. It was crazy. There was zero proof. My parents came in and threatened to sue the school. They backed off, and things quieted down for a couple of days for me when they started to question Debbie. Then, out of the blue, Mr. Culver came to her rescue, saying Debbie had told him I had gotten a copy of the test. He was lying to protect her. Debbie was Mr. C's pet."

"It's a long time ago, way past any statute of limitations, and I'm curious, did you find a way to get a copy of the test?"

"No."

"I understand you did really well on the test, better than you were expected to, causing the school to believe you had gotten an advance copy. How do you explain the difference in scores when they made you retake the test?"

"Forcing me to take another test was bullshit. I did good on the first one. There was no particular reason. I had taken SAT prep courses and felt good on the first one. When I had to do it over again, I was nervous and stressed out. The test seemed harder, and I didn't do as good."

That was an understatement. His score was a hundred points lower.

"If what you say about Boyle being interested in you but you not in her is true, I can understand why Boyle could have been looking for revenge. But what I can't figure out is why a teacher would support the allegation against you."

"Mr. C was a good guy. All the kids liked him, especially the girls. He didn't say I did anything. He only said that Debbie told him I stole a copy of the test."

Something for me to look into. "Okay, I understand. The school couldn't suspend you without proof and made you take it over."

"There was no proof, but by forcing me to take another test they were saying I was guilty."

"You must have been upset. Who wants to take another four-hour test?"

"It was a nightmare."

"I understand you threatened her."

His shoulder's sagged. "Look, I was pissed off. The entire school was talking about it. My parents and family supported me, but you could see they weren't convinced I didn't do it. They kept asking me about it over and over."

"But you did threaten her."

He nodded.

"According to a witness, you said something like you'd get her for this, that she'd pay for what she did to you."

"I don't remember what I said; it was twenty-five years ago."

"You left Naples right after Debbie Boyle was murdered."

"You make it seem like I ran away. I didn't run away. I went to college in Richmond, Virginia."

"Classes didn't start at the University of Richmond until late August, yet you left Naples the first week of June."

"I was anxious to get started, that's all. Ever since the SAT test nonsense, things changed for me. Naples was a small community back then, especially the school system; people talked about me."

"A friend of Debbie's said that you wanted to cut the brake line in her car."

"I was just spouting off, that's all. It's not a crime to say stupid things."

"You never came back to Naples after school. Why was that?"

"Are you kidding me? You think I had something to do with her death?" He got up. "This is crazy. I'm sorry, but I don't believe I should continue this conversation without a lawyer."

Twenty-five years later, the uproar over a stolen test would fade as motivation for murder for most people. But Moore was a teenager, only seventeen at the time. Plus, up in New Jersey, I had seen my share of killings over parking spots, phones, and even a Yankee cap. The embarrassment and disgrace a young man would feel could easily morph into murderous rage.

Chapter 19

No need for a clock, my stomach was telling me it was almost six o'clock; time to finish up and go home. Derrick had been out all day interviewing, and the court system wasted another of my days. It burned me up, all the legal maneuvering that defense attorneys used to delay and divert attention from their clients.

Given my experience in the Barrow case, I was a bigger proponent than most of the innocent until proven guilty principle. The problem is, we'd allowed the lawyers to abuse the system with tactic after tactic, motion after motion. It was maddening to sit, in this case over five hours, including lunch, to testify.

How was justice served? A defendant is entitled to a credible defense, but how was the public served by having its law enforcement officers sit on their hands in a courtroom? There had to be a better way of scheduling witnesses, for both sides.

Adding to my frustration was the fact the handbag thieves hadn't come back to Waterside Shops. I'd scared them off. I had a decision to make regarding continuing the surveillance. Should I kill it entirely? Cut it back? I wanted to catch the bastards, but Mary Ann reminded me last night that I was making it personal.

The gang had never used or even shown a weapon during their grab-and-run stunts. They were brazen, but Saks was a soft target. They wanted to harden the department by securing expensive bags with wire tethers. I'd asked them to hold off, knowing if they did, the handbag ring would move on, terrorizing another town.

It wasn't personal; this was a criminal enterprise that had to be stopped. We couldn't allow Naples to turn into Chicago or Baltimore, where mobs storm stores, stealing and running. I was going to continue the surveillance, though cut it back a bit, and catch these bastards.

As I tapped out a new surveillance order, Derrick came in wearing a frown and a blue tie. I asked, "How'd you make out?"

"Nothing. Total waste of time. Nobody could ID Boralis."

"Not even a maybe?"

"Zippo. It's frustrating not being able to advance the case."

"You did. Eliminating someone who was luring young girls helps focus the investigation."

"Yeah? How come I feel like I pissed away a day?"

"You? Try sitting in a court all day. My ass is killing me."

"You got no ass to hurt."

He was right; I had no ass, but that wasn't what hit me. It was the fact our relationship had just moved a step forward. The kid was comfortable breaking my chops.

"Your observation skills are first-rate, Detective. Now, get back to work."

"How about that message from Interpol saying they had something on Papadakis and were compiling a report?"

"It could be anything, but I asked a buddy of mine with the FBI to see what he could come up with. In the meantime, why don't you dig into Papadakis. Learn as much as we can about him. He's been here a long time and had to leave a trail if he's our guy."

"Who knows, there could be bodies we know nothing about."

"I don't know about that, but there are hundreds of cases of missing teenagers each year. They run away for different reasons, some end up being abused but some are killed."

"You think he may have killed before, and the bodies not discovered?"

"We don't know that he's ever killed, no less again. That's why we have to get a better grip on who he is."

"I'm on it, boss."

* * *

I couldn't catch a whiff of anything cooking, and Mary Ann was in a recliner watching the news. "Hey, babe. What are you making for dinner? I'm starved."

"You said you wanted to go out tonight."

I did? "Oh, yeah. What do you feel like?"

"You pick it."

"Let's try that place: Black Jack Pizza."

"You heard it's good? It looks like nothing from the outside."

"I love the name. It's gotta be good."

"Just like that Iguana Mia place? You liked the name on that one too, remember?"

"Thanks for reminding me. You know what? It's such a nice night, let's take a run down to Docs in Bonita. You ready to roll? I'm really hungry."

"Sure, let me get my bag."

"Speaking of bags, I was thinking to cut the surveillance team down at Saks."

"You're not going to end it?"

"Why not give it another week or so? See if the bad guys come back."

We headed to the garage. "Be careful, Frank. They never came less than a dozen strong."

"I know, but we only need one undercover sales girl, a camera monitor, and one unmarked."

"That's too light."

"I was thinking, as soon as we see them on camera, we call for help. We can put an end to this."

"Just as easy to have Saks tether the bags, like they wanted to. You catch them or not, Saks is going to put the security locks on anyway."

I hit the garage door opener. "You're missing it, Mary Ann. We got to lock these bastards up, send a message out that we're not going to let you get away with anything."

"I get it, Frank, but you always preach about allocation of resources, and to me this is not the best choice, okay?"

"I want to shut these guys down, that's all. I think we can do it with a skinny team."

Backing out of the driveway, she said, "Just don't let it get personal."

It was personal. I screwed up, and I needed to straighten the score out. "Don't worry."

"Anything new on the Boyle case?"

"A lot of possibilities. Some people of interest could have been ruled out but not documented. I don't want to bad-mouth a brother officer, but this looks like a textbook case on what not to do."

"What about that deathbed confession call?"

"He had another alibi that's shakier than a palm frond. I'm going back to see him in the next day or two."

Chapter 20

There were a couple of young kids riding bikes in the cul-de-sac, confirming my belief Delasol was a full-timer community. The smell of fresh-cut grass caught the back of my throat, and I hacked an "ahem" as Lew Mackay opened the door.

His white skin was punctuated by a pimple or a bug bite in the center of his forehead. After scanning over my shoulder, Mackay's puckered look receded a bit.

"Please, come on in, Detective."

I stepped forward silently.

"Can I get you anything?"

I shook my head.

"Did you get the chance to see Hector?"

"Yes, we went to see your boy Machado."

His eyes shifted. "He backed up what I told you, right?"

"Not exactly."

"What do you mean? I'm telling the truth."

"You sure you don't want to tell me what you were doing at Delnor-Wiggins the night Debbie Boyle was murdered?"

"I'm telling you, man. I didn't do it. I had nothing to do with it. I was delivering cash to someone."

"You expect me to believe you were involved with a drug dealer like Hector Machado? You think it's like working for Uber; you're in when you want?"

"That *is* what it was. I needed money. I was in a hole, and I had to do something."

"So, you decided to be a money mule?"

"I was desperate. I knew a guy who made easy money that way, and he introduced me to a friend of Machado's."

"Who was this friend?"

"Mike Conner."

"Where can I find Conner?"

Mackay frowned. "I know it sounds bad, but he's dead. Died in a car accident about ten years ago."

I was sick of hearing alibis involving dead men. "Give me his last known address."

Mackay didn't hesitate, and I jotted down what he gave me. I could poke around and find out if this Conner had a history.

"I still don't understand what Hector told you. It's the truth. I was working for him."

"Machado said he didn't know you. I showed him your picture, and he couldn't identify you. You'd think he'd remember someone he'd entrusted a bag of money to."

"It was a long time ago, and I wore a wig, with long hair and a baseball cap. I was afraid someone would recognize me."

"Someone did. That's why I'm here."

"No, I wore it when I met Hector at the Pewter Mug. That's where he gave me the money and told me where to meet his contact."

Mackay wasn't someone you could trust. That was clear. He had zero principles, deciding to engage in drug dealing because he was short on cash as easily as deciding where to eat. Despite my intense dislike for him, I found myself believing what he said about the disguise.

"What color wig? What length?"

"Black, down to about here." He touched his upper shoulder. "It was something I bought at the Spencer Gifts store, that used to be in the Coastland Mall."

"What kind of baseball cap?"

"Dallas Cowboys."

Not a football fan, I couldn't recall if they were America's Team back in 1993. "Did you wear the same getup every time?"

"Yeah. But I only did it twice."

Oh, you only engaged in drug dealing twice? No problem, a judge would understand.

"I'm going to look into what you've told me, and I gotta warn you:

if you're jerking me around, wasting time I don't have, the next time you see me I'll be slapping cuffs on you."

* * *

Easing into my day with a second cup of coffee, I leafed through the *Forensic Monthly Journal*. I read a small article on an interesting advance in biomechanics. Using computers, technicians would feed information about a wound into a high-powered program. The program would analyze the data and build graphics, recreating scenarios of how the wound was inflicted.

The information was valuable in determining the height of an attacker, from which direction they came, and more importantly, was able to discern between an accidental fall and intentional injury.

I typed in a link the article mentioned to view real-world examples of the technology in action. The first video dealt with a fatal stabbing, the defense contending the victim had fallen on a knife while cooking.

An animated drawing of the woman, complete with dangling earrings, came to life. In slow motion, the figure fell toward the floor, holding a kitchen knife. Collapsing, the knife disappeared under the woman. A view from underneath showed that the angle of the arm made it impossible for the stab wound to have occurred while falling.

When a second animation began, a man entered the screen, arm cocked, holding a knife. The woman backed away from her attacker, stumbling as the knife was plunged into her chest. Close-ups of the wound area matched the angle of the actual wound. It was a compelling display.

It was a good thing I was in my early forties, because technology was going to be shrinking the detective employment rolls. I signed up to be notified for when a class was being held in the area. It would make me less dependent on a moody coroner and make a powerful impression in a courtroom.

An idea on a possible use of the technology hit me as my partner came into the office.

"Morning, boss."

Derrick set a Dunkin' Donuts cup on my desk. "Thanks. You

should check out this piece on biomechanicals. It's amazing; the realistic graphics that can be created. They say it's a science. I don't know about that, but the recreations can reveal a lot about how a wound occurred."

"Maybe we can use it on the Boyle case. She had multiple wounds. Maybe we can learn something."

"It's not the stab wounds I'm interested in. It's the head injury the boyfriend Wheeler said he suffered."

"You mean whether it was self-inflicted or not?"

"Bingo."

"You think biomechanics could help?"

"Why not? Only thing is, we're dealing with twenty-five-year-old pictures. I'm hoping there's enough to go on."

"Who would be able to analyze them?"

"Not sure yet, but I'll find out. Meanwhile, tell me what you dug up on Papadakis."

Chapter 21

Derrick was filling me in.

"I wish I had more, but Papadakis has either laid low for a quarter of a century or is the smartest killer in history. He's worked at the same accounting firm for over twenty years. He's not an accountant, but from what they told me, a high-level bookkeeper."

"That would mean he's detail-oriented, would know he'd need to cover his tracks. What kind of clients has he worked for?"

"Uh, I didn't ask."

"It could be important information. Gives us a wider network to make connections. Who knows, maybe one of his clients has gone missing."

"You think so?"

"No, but it's something we need to know. What about neighbors, friends?"

"Nothing. He's a loner, but everyone said he never caused trouble and wasn't prone to anger."

"Loner? That's interesting. Most killers are loners."

"What should we do next with him?"

"Check his roster of clients. If nothing comes up, leave it until we hear from the feds."

"Okay. I'll get right on it."

"Also, I need you to interview Machado, the guy Mackay said he was muling cash for."

Derrick was on his feet. "Sure. You saw him once, right?"

"Yes, with Detective Vargas. He's at a halfway joint in Immokalee. Machado has been in and out of prison his entire life. You okay going alone?"

"No problem. Up in DC I was around these so-called tough guys all the time. What's the mission?"

I explained what Mackay had told me regarding his disguise.

Derrick headed for the door. "I got it. Don't worry."

I pointed to his jacket, which was hung over the back of his chair and said, "I know you do."

* * *

Tamiami Trail was deserted. I had the windows down as I made my way to Hodges University. Their Naples campus, close to the intersection of Immokalee and I-75, was as convenient as it could get. I didn't know what was shining brighter, the sun or my optimism that a biomechanical professor would clarify Wheeler's injury.

Hodges had a growing criminal justice program and had lured Joseph Liston, a professor of biomechanics, from Chicago. I pulled up to a handful of beige, two-story buildings. The place looked more like a corporate headquarters than a college campus.

Grabbing my bag, I followed a meandering sidewalk to the main building. A couple of twenty-somethings, wearing Santa hats, were camped under a magnolia tree near the entrance. Even though I'd been down in Naples for a couple of years, I still couldn't get used to eighty-degree weather with Christmas two weeks away.

Joe Liston had bushy eyebrows and enough hair growing out of his ears to give me the heebie-jeebies. His blue eyes were intense, and he firmly shook my hand.

"Nice to meet you, Detective."

"Same here, Professor. I really appreciate you taking the time to help me."

"No problem. I worked with the Chicago PD all the time."

"That's a busy place to be a cop."

"A part of Chicago is a war zone. It's a damn shame. How can I help you?"

"I've got this case: it's cold, from 1993. A seventeen-year-old girl was murdered at Wiggins Park. She was there with her seven-year-old brother and her twenty-two-year-old boyfriend. Sometime around eight she said she had to go to the bathroom and left her brother and boyfriend behind. She never returned. The boyfriend left the younger boy, saying he was going to look for her. The boyfriend claims he was attacked and knocked unconscious. The girl was found dead several hours later. These are old, but this is what I'm working with."

I slid pictures of Debbie Boyle's body across Davidson's desk. Professor Davidson studied each picture slowly and used a magnifying glass on two of the five pictures.

"You're trying to determine what, Detective? The killer's dominant hand? The weapon?"

"No, no. The boyfriend's story is just a little too convenient. He claims to have no recollection of events that night, and a subsequent interview revealed certain inconsistencies. Take a look at these."

I handed three Polaroids of the forehead wound Wheeler claimed was inflicted by an outsider. "Is there any way you could determine if this was self-inflicted?"

Davidson examined the pictures and said, "Were any X-rays taken at the time?"

"It's unbelievable, but no."

"That's unfortunate." He picked up a photo again. "It'd be difficult without knowing the weapon used."

"Can you try?"

"Sure, but a simple way to determine the force of a blow like this would be brain swelling and skull fracturing. You see, it's not impossible, but let me show you. Stand up for a moment. Is your dominant side right or left?"

"I'm right-handed."

"Okay, take this ruler in your right hand. Now, extend your arm and move toward it forward as if to strike your forehead."

It was an awkward move.

"You see, the force of a blow is limited by the short range your elbow allows."

"Oh, I can feel how limiting that is."

"Now, you'd get more momentum by holding the ends with each hand and bringing it toward your forehand. Using that maneuver allows your elbows to get more range, they end up in back of you. Of course, another way to self-inflict a forehead wound would be to strike your head against an object, say a wall, or in this case, a branch or fence railing. But that is also a movement with limited range."

I tossed my head back and swung it forward, my chin hitting my chest. "Would any of these self-inflicted moves cause someone to lose consciousness?"

"It would be difficult, but for someone with previous head injuries, like a concussion, it is possible."

"Do you think taking a closer look would help clarify things?"

"I have a suggestion." Liston sat back down. "We have instinctual reactions that serve to protect the body. As much as we might plan, to say, strike our head against a brick wall as hard as possible, our subconscious will mitigate the force we apply."

"Softening the blow?"

"Exactly."

"So what next?"

"An MRI. Today's technology should be able to detect even the slightest, say a hairline fracture, that's healed. If there was evidence of a fracture, especially a significant one, it would be compelling evidence that he was struck by a force outside his control."

"That's a good idea. I just don't know if we can get him to voluntarily submit to a test like that."

Liston shrugged. "Can't help there."

"You've been very helpful, Professor, very helpful."

Explaining the purpose of an MRI and Wheeler's reaction to one would reveal plenty about how he got the injury. A rush of excitement made it hard to resist skipping back to my car.

Chapter 22

I dug in my pocket for my office key before realizing the door was open. I checked the time. It was only eight fifteen, and Derrick was behind his desk with a big smile.

"Morning, boss. I got you a coffee, on the dark side."

I nodded. "Thanks."

"You're never going to believe it, but Interpol sent in a report on Papadakis."

I needed to ease into a day. It took two coffees to get me ready to function. I picked up the cup on my desk. "Whoa. How long you been here? The coffee's just about cold."

"Around seven. I was up at five and checked my email. Once I saw the Interpol report, I couldn't get back to sleep."

I took a gulp of the lukewarm coffee as Derrick struggled to stay in his skin. "All right, tell me, what did you get from Interpol?"

Derrick popped out of his seat. "Our boy Papadakis was a suspect in a death in Greece."

The news hit me like a shot of Red Bull. "Who was the victim?"

"Another teenager, but a boy this time."

"Was there any connection between Papadakis and the kid?"

Derrick swiped a document off his desk and passed it to me. "This is what they sent."

There wasn't much. The Hellenic Police had reported Papadakis to Interpol in April of 1987 to prevent him from fleeing Greece. Papadakis was a person of interest in the stabbing death of Spiro Xeanax, a sixteen-year-old boy from a town I couldn't pronounce. They eventually lifted the travel ban, but the murder remained unsolved.

"Did you see? It was another stabbing."

"Yes, but a male victim."

"I didn't know what to do next. How do we get more on this?"

"Good question. I'm not sure what the Greeks even kept on this. They might have tossed it; it's over thirty years ago."

"They can't do that, can they?"

"Probably not."

I couldn't even imagine looking into another decades-old murder, especially one that happened in Greece. What would be the proper course of action? It was tough to admit, but I had no idea where to start. With Interpol? The Greek police? Maybe the state department?

Maybe my new buddy Haines would know. He was with the FBI, which didn't get involved internationally, but I was betting he had some ideas and a contact or two. It was worth a shot before going to Sheriff Chester. If he knew I was looking into a murder five thousand miles away, he'd probably tell me to drop the entire Boyle investigation.

* * *

Derrick had confirmed that Fred Jones was Gerry Moore's best friend in high school. We turned into Bear Creek, and I flashed a badge at the gate. Derrick said, "Bear Creek? In Florida? What kind of name is that?"

"You'd be surprised how many black bears are in the county."

"Really? I thought they were up in the Northeast mountain areas."

"I thought the same thing, but black bears are up and down the entire East Coast. I've seen three so far."

"Wow. I'd love to see one."

We pulled up to a coach home with a red-orange tile roof in need of a power wash. The home, whose landscaping was overgrown, looked about thirty years old. I put a three-hundred-thousand-dollar price tag on it. There was a smell of curry in the air. I hoped it wasn't coming from Jones's place.

Fred Jones's head was tilted back like he was looking over your head. Ugh, I could see the hairs in his nose. He enveloped my hand—another guy in better shape than I was.

"You know, I'm a big fan of the police. My uncle was a cop up in Indiana. Man, I idolized him growing up."

Always suspicious when someone praises us. I smiled. "Thanks."

He led us into a family room, three shades too dark for me. A baseball game was playing on the tube.

"Devil Rays against the Yanks."

Derrick said, "They're called just the Rays now."

"Just another example of politically correct nonsense. I mean, who was offended by the devil?"

"Crazy. Ain't it?"

"How about a bottle of water?"

"Sure."

He went into the kitchen. "So, you're looking into the old Boyle murder."

I glared at Derrick, but he shook his head. I said, "You talked with Gerry Moore?"

"Yeah, we usually talk every couple of weeks, you know, catch up."

He handed me a bottle of Poland Springs. "What did he tell you?"

"That you went to see him and were asking questions, like he could have been the one to kill Debbie."

Derrick said, "What do you think?"

"About what?"

"About the possibility your friend Gerry did it."

"Gerry? I can't imagine him doing something like that."

I said, "The two of you were good friends in high school, correct?"

"Yeah, we were best friends. Still are, really."

"I'm interested to hear more about the SAT test incident."

"He told me you were grilling him on it. But I get it; you got a job to do."

Derrick said, "Do you think he stole the test?"

"No way. If he did he would have offered it to me. We both were terrified of taking the exam. What kid isn't?"

"Did he ever mention trying to get an advantage of some sort?"

"Where would he get a copy from?"

"But he did very well on the test."

"Trust me, I was surprised, but he took prep classes. We all did. To say it was because he stole a copy was crazy."

"When he was accused, how did he react?"

"He was pissed, man. There was all this drama at the school, and he was at the center of it. He even said his parents thought he'd done it when it first happened."

"Why do you think Debbie Boyle would say something like that?"

"I don't have a clue."

"Gerry said she was coming on to him, and when he rejected her she got mad."

"I don't know about that. He said that, but in all honesty, I never saw her go after him."

"We understand the controversy died down after she made the allegation but had no proof."

"Yeah, it went away after about two weeks. But then Mr. Culver, he was the hot teacher back then, backed her up when he said Debbie had told him about it."

"Do you think the teacher was lying?"

He shook his head. "No, I don't think he would do something like that, but all he said was that she had told him about it. He never said Gerry did anything."

"We know that Gerry threatened Debbie Boyle, saying he'd make her pay for what she did."

"He was just trying to scare her, you know. Make himself look tough."

"Moore left Naples right after Boyle was murdered."

"He went away to college, down in Richmond. I don't remember when exactly, but it wasn't right after. I know he went earlier than I did, but he was anxious for a change, and a friend of his brother's had an apartment where we stayed until the dorms opened up."

"Moore never came back to Naples. Any particular reason?"

"He came back; his family was here. He found a job up in Sarasota. It's only two hours away."

"Moore said he was with you the night Debbie Boyle was murdered."

"Yeah, we were together. He slept over that night."

"But your parents weren't home, right?"

"They went up to Tampa."

"And no one else was there?"

"No, just the two of us."

"What did you do that night?"

"We watched *The Godfather* twice, then *The Night of the Living Dead*. Had pizza and some beers."

"You remember what you watched twenty-five years ago?"

"Yeah. First off, it was the night Debbie died, and we both loved movies, especially *The Godfather*."

"You wouldn't be protecting your friend with an alibi, would you?"

"No, no way. We're best friends, but I'd never do something like that. That's against the law, isn't it?"

"Obstruction of justice."

We finished up, and as soon as we got in the car, Derrick said, "The whole bit about watching movies with Moore seems fishy."

"I don't know."

"His parents were away, and no one else to verify it. Don't you think it's a little too convenient?"

"That's because he's telling the truth."

"How could you say that?"

"The file said the parents verified they were away. That would mean that they planned the murder together, knowing they'd have an alibi."

"Okay."

"But they never could have known that Boyle would be at Wiggins the same night."

"Oh, I didn't think it through."

"You made an error when we started out with Jones. When we conduct an interview we plant seeds, box in a witness. You started right out asking him if he thought Moore killed Boyle."

"Why was that a mistake?"

"You wait for that moment, building up to it, seeing if the witness hints at or outright tells us something that would conflict with that assumption. You ruined the opportunity to ask Jones questions about Moore, like if he was violent, for example."

"We could have asked that."

"But he was on guard. He already said no way his buddy could have done it. You see what I'm saying? There's a psychological dance we have to do. Be careful, and if in doubt, keep quiet."

It wasn't easy sitting next to a sulking man, but I was doing it for his own good.

Chapter 23

Grabbing my coat and the keys to the Cherokee, I left the office to pay another visit with Clem Walker, the fisherman, another guy whose story didn't quite line up.

I knew there were die-hard guys who surf-fished. In fact, there was one guy who was casting every single time I went to the beach. This guy wore a hat with scores of bird feathers he'd collected off the beach. There was another guy with poor posture who was there just about every day as well. I'd chatted with both of them a couple of times, and they had nothing in common with Walker.

I knew it a was a small sampling to make a judgment, but Walker also didn't have a bucket with him. I spoke with a dozen guys down at Naples City Dock, and every one of them said they never fished without a bucket of some type. Besides, Walker lived on Capri Island, which looked like a boater's paradise to me. Why the hell would he drive all the way to Wiggins? At night? It'd take him twenty-five minutes each way.

Approaching Marco Island, I made a right onto Capri Island. A salty breeze swept through my Cherokee as I pulled up to Walker's house. His boat and red pickup were in the same position. The sea smell gave way to a smoky odor that I thought was cedar.

He didn't answer the door, but I saw a figure out back and walked around the side of the blue house. Wearing cutoffs, Walker was standing in front of a barrel-shaped BBQ. Smoke was pouring out of the sides of the grill.

"Mr. Walker?"

Cigarette dangling from his mouth, Walker turned around. "Oh, hang on minute. Almost done here."

"You making lunch?"

"Nah, I'm smoking some local swordfish."

Swordfish? "I never did anything like that. Are you using cedar?"

Walker crushed his cigarette out in the gravel. "Yep. It's easy. You just got to cure the fish first, I use a bunch of spices and salts my granddaddy taught me to use. Then you let it dry. It forms a kinda glaze on it to keep the moisture in and bacteria out. After that, you're ready to smoke it."

He lifted the lid and a cloud of smoke enveloped his head. I ducked away from the smoke as he said, "This baby's done. As soon as she cools down, I'll wrap it up. Unless you want some."

Never tasting any smoked fish besides salmon and whiting, I wanted some, but the concern about the home's refrigeration, and the fishy smell turned me off.

"Thanks, I'll pass. Maybe next time."

"Mind if we talk out here?" He motioned toward a set of outdoor furniture that I had looked at myself at Costco.

"Works for me." There weren't any cushions on the chairs, hurting my bony ass.

Walker sat opposite me and lit another cigarette.

"I'll get right to it, then. I can't see why anyone who lives out here and has a boat would drive to Wiggins Park to fish, especially at night."

"I prefer surf-fishing; it's more challenging, you know, plus you get to walk the beach, get the sand 'tween your toes."

I had to agree on the sand assessment. "Don't you go fishing on your boat?"

"No, never."

"Never?"

Walker picked a piece of tobacco off his tongue. "Yeah, never."

"I may not know a lot about fishing, but I know you can't catch a swordfish from the beach."

"That's right. They're big-assed fish."

"So, where'd you catch it, off your boat?"

"Nah, my neighbor, one house down, bagged it."

Good answer and easy to check. "Gotcha. Now, I checked, and you have a record."

"So? It's penny-ante stuff."

"Maybe the pot charges, but I wouldn't call assaulting your neighbor penny ante."

Walker took a long drag, tilted his head and blew the smoke skyward. "That bastard was out of line."

"So, you put him in the hospital with five broken ribs and a concussion?"

"He deserved it, and it made the pig move away."

"Just what ticked you off?"

"It was over a long period of time. He kept being a jerk. But one weekend, my niece Nadeen was over. She was only twelve at the time. I had a Boston Whaler, and she wanted to wash it, so we were out in the driveway, and he came around and started to hit on her. She was a kid, and I told him to knock it off. He left, but not before cursing and making a really lewd comment. I went after him but just warned him. Then, later that night, we had a BBQ and were out here playing cards, and he started shooting off fireworks. The rockets were going all over, and I asked him to cut it out. He stops for five minutes and then starts aiming the rockets at us. One almost hit Nadeen, and I flipped out."

The neighbor sounded like he needed the beating. "You could've called the police."

"Believe me, I wish I did. My sister wouldn't let Nadeen visit me for five years."

"You claimed that you were the one that suggested calling the police when Debbie Boyle went missing."

"That's right. I didn't know what to make of what was going on. The boyfriend was worked up, saying he had been attacked, and there was the kid."

"But you never called, yourself."

Walker fingered another cigarette and said, "If it were today and I had a cell phone I would've."

Ending the interview, I declined another offer of smoked fish and headed to the front of the house.

I walked to the driveway. The boat was backed up to but not hooked up to the truck. Its interior was littered with leaves, and the boat's trailer had a flat tire. How did I miss that? Maybe this Walker *was* just out fishing. If it weren't for the bucket thing, I'd totally clear him.

Heading north on 75, I passed the Rattlesnake Hammock exit and my phone rang.

"Frank, it's Tom Haines."

"How you doing, Tommy?"

"Good. Wanted to give you a heads-up. I'm sending over what we dug up on Igor Papadakis."

"Thanks. Anything interesting?"

"Guy looks like Peter Frampton."

Frampton? Papadakis? "What are you talking about? Guy's got black hair."

"Picture of him with long blond hair, wavy, like Frampton had way back then before he went bald."

Blond hair? The beach walker, Nielsen, said she saw a blond-haired woman at the park. Could it have been Papadakis?

Chapter 24

My mind and the Cherokee racing, I made my way to the office. Would Diane Nielsen recognize a picture of Papadakis with his blond hair as the person she noticed at Delnor-Wiggins? Were there any blond hairs at the crime scene that could have been Papadakis's? I should have known better and checked, instead of assuming they came from the victim.

Was I no better than the amateurs who handled the case? The chemo I'd taken had done a number on me, and none of the brain exercises or supplements seemed to be working.

Derrick leapt up when I stormed in.

"Hey, Frank, just got back from seeing Machado."

I made the T sign with my hands. "Hold on. The FBI sent me a file on Papadakis."

"That's perfect, because Machado put the squash on Mackay."

My computer was taking too long to boot up. "What did he say?"

"Said he remembered the guy was wearing a baseball cap—"

"How did he remember that?"

"He said the guy was wearing it real low, tugged all the way down."

I hit the email icon. "Plenty of guys wore caps back then."

"He knew it was a Cowboys hat."

I turned around. "How would he know that?"

"I never mentioned the type of cap. I asked him if he remembered, and he told me it was a Cowboys hat. He said he was a big Packers fan, and they lost to the Cowboys in the Super Bowl that year. Machado said he hates the Cowboys."

"But he couldn't say for sure it was Mackay."

"No, but I tend to believe it was Mackay."

The email from Haines was the third one down. I clicked on it and said, "Dig into Mackay's finances. See if you can find him paying off a loan or getting current on one. Track down his landlord, things like that. Find out if he was suddenly flush with cash. Oh, and find out from Machado and Mackay how much he got for the runs. See if that jibes."

The email opened, revealing two attachments and a short message: Hi Frank, here you go. Good Luck, Tom.

I clicked the JPG extension, and a picture of a man bearing little resemblance to Papadakis stared back at me. I didn't see Peter Frampton in the face, but the hair was blond, wavy, and shoulder length.

Derrick was looking over my shoulder. "Holy shit, he's got blond hair. Maybe he's the one that beach walker mentioned."

He had to know I already thought of that. "When Haines called me, I thought the same thing."

"Are we sure that's Papadakis?"

"This picture is over thirty years old. Let me get something to compare it with."

My pee-pee alarm rang as I pulled up Papadakis's DMV photo. The shoe-polish black threw me off, but the eyes were the same distance apart and their color matched. His chin had fattened, rounding his face, but that is what three decades of gravity will do. The nose in the DMV picture was slightly wider, beefier, but close enough. The more I studied the images the closer they appeared. No need to run it through the facial simulator.

"It's him. Let's see what they have on him."

* * *

Wheeler didn't want me to come over again. He gave me a hard time on the phone, making me suspicious. There was no way he was going to blow me off. I pressed him, and he caved.

Wearing a broad smile, Wheeler greeted me like an old friend, causing my bullshit meter to buzz. It could have been the stubble on his face, but he looked tired and older. Was something keeping him up at night?

"Come on in. Good to see you again."

I stepped in as Wheeler slid a couple of plastic tools to the side.

"Sorry. My kid hasn't learned to put his toys away."

For some reason I was jealous of Wheeler, having a kid to play with and teach. I hadn't thought about being a father much, but recently it had crept into my thoughts.

"It must be nice to have a son."

"Oh, it's unreal. He's amazing, but it's not all good. When he gets a temper tantrum you don't want to be around. You got kids?"

"Nah. The window's closing in on me."

"Get moving. Trust me, you haven't lived until you have kids."

Thanks, I really needed that. "We'll see."

"Come on, we'll sit out back, like the last time."

"Sounds good."

As we passed the kitchen, he said, "I'll grab us something to drink. Water okay?"

"Perfect."

He handed me a bottle of water and popped the top off a can of root beer. He took a slug and said, "How is the case going?"

"That's why I'm here. I went to see Clem Walker, the guy who was fishing that night. He's positive that it was his idea to call the police."

"That's not the way I remember it. I was confused; it was crazy; my head hurt. Debbie was missing, and I needed help, so that's why I wanted the police."

"But you went looking for her first."

"Of course we did. She was missing. We looked around hoping we'd find her."

"But if you were attacked, like you said, there was someone dangerous out there. Why not get the police?"

"I *was* attacked. There were two of us, plus her brother, to confront anyone."

"Can you understand how your version of events, that you were attacked and knocked unconscious, but not seriously enough to, say, require medical attention, sounds a little too convenient?"

"I went to the hospital and was admitted."

"That was for observation. You were released the next morning."

"So, you'd be happier if I had a serious injury? Maybe lost an eye or something?"

"What would clear this up would be some way to prove that you were struck by an unknown assailant; the same person who murdered Boyle."

"How can we prove that now?"

"An MRI."

"An MRI? Why?"

"It would show whether you had a hairline fracture that healed and whether any other damage was suffered."

"I can't believe it would show after up all these years."

"So, you'll agree to get an MRI?"

"I'd like to, really, I would, but that's a significant dose of radiation I'd get. It wouldn't be good for me. My doctor advised me that, with my family history of cancer, I shouldn't get an X-ray, CAT scan, or MRI unless it's absolutely necessary."

It was an excuse that seemed absurd on the surface. More proof that if you stick around long enough you'll see everything. I'd have a talk with his doctor to see if he was lying to me.

Chapter 25

I slammed the phone down. "What bullshit!"

Derrick said, "What's the matter, Frank?"

"Wheeler's doctor won't give me any information about Wheeler or his family history. Said it's confidential."

"But we just need to know if he advised him not to be exposed to tests involving radiation."

"I know. This woman said they were sued in the past for inadvertently releasing records and said we'd have to get a court order."

"You going to ask the DA for one?"

"Not yet. I'm gonna give it another try. Go see the doctor at his home."

"Why don't we talk to Wheeler's wife?"

"She'd lie to protect the father of her child, but it might be worth a shot. You want to do the honors? I'm going to see Debbie Boyle's mother again."

He jumped up and grabbed his jacket. "I'm on it."

Derrick bumped into Vargas as she was coming in the door.

"Oh, sorry, Mary Ann."

"It's okay. How you doing?"

"Great. Look, I gotta run. Frank wants me to interview someone."

Vargas called after him, "Don't speed."

"You got him all worked up, Frank."

"He'll survive."

"How's he doing? Seems like you two are a good match."

"He's okay. A good kid, but I'm not sure about his instincts."

"But you said he surprised you a couple of times with his line of questioning."

"Derrick's okay, but he's no JJ. Man, JJ could look at a suspect and do a mental autopsy. He was something. One of a kind, that's for sure."

"Give Derrick a chance to develop. I'll bet you two will be inseparable in less than a year."

"We'll work together, but that's it. I'm not getting close, like I did with JJ. Losing him was, well, it hurt too much. I'm not letting that happen again."

"Frank, you're talking like a child. You don't open yourself up, you'll never experience the good in people. Besides, what about me? You got close to me, didn't you?"

"That's different."

"No, it's not. We took a chance on each other, opening ourselves up. It could go wrong someday, though I don't think it will. What would have happened if one of us was afraid to open up?"

Why did she have to bring all this up? I didn't want to be worrying about Derrick's life. I liked it the way it was: only worrying about Mary Ann, me, and catching killers.

"I'd probably be at the bar in Campiello's."

She punched my shoulder. "Yeah, right. I hate to tell you, but you're not exactly a sugar daddy."

"Damn, I always wanted to see what it was like getting attacked by a cougar."

"You keep it up, and you'll get the chance."

"You want to take a ride?"

"Where?"

"To see Debbie Boyle's mother."

"I don't think I should. Take Derrick, he needs the experience."

"But I need a woman's touch with her."

"It wouldn't be fair to him."

"What are you talking about? We still have time. Chester gave us ninety days to wind it down."

"But I haven't done anything on the case in weeks."

"I know, but it'd be fun to work together again. Like old times."

"It doesn't feel right, Frank."

"We'll go to lunch somewhere close to her house and say we were in the neighborhood or something like that."

"Why make up an excuse? You know better than that."

"You're right. It was stupid. Forget the whole thing. I'll go myself. See you later."

Chapter 26

Cathy Boyle was holding a dish towel when she opened the door. The shoulder line of her marine blue dress was punctuated on each end by boney points. Her steely eyes had softened, and she seemed glad to see me.

"It's good to see you, Detective Luca."

"Same here, Mrs. Boyle."

"I meant to say it the first time I saw you, but you bear a striking resemblance to George Clooney."

"And as you know, you and your daughter could have passed for twins."

She smiled. "Come on in. Let me get rid of this towel."

We sat on the same couches, but I noticed the party dress picture of her daughter had been replaced with one of her in a cheerleading outfit. There wasn't anything in the room that would signal Christmas was around the corner. I smelled coffee and hoped she'd offer me a cup.

"You know, I'm kind of surprised that you're still interested in my daughter's case. Over the years I've had a few calls about the case, raising my hopes, but there was never any follow-up."

"I can't promise you more than my commitment to do everything I can to bring Debbie's killer to justice."

She looked into my eyes for a moment before saying, "That's all I ever wanted. Thank you. Oh, I just made a pot of coffee. Would you like a cup?"

"Yes, please. No sugar and just a splash of milk."

She handed me a blue mug of coffee that had too much milk in it. I forced a thank you, placed it on the table, and took my Moleskine out.

"I'd like you to tell me everything you remember from the night before, up to the time Debbie went to Delnor-Wiggins Park."

She sipped her coffee and said, "Believe me, I've relived that day a thousand times. The night before was pretty standard for the kids. I grilled some hamburgers for dinner and we ate out back. Brian was finished with school for the year and was watching TV. I had a wedding the next day, so Debbie was helping me decide what jewelry and shoes to wear." She frowned. "I really miss the girlie things we did together."

"What kind of mood was Debbie in that night?"

"She was quieter than usual. I asked her if everything was all right. She said nothing was wrong, so I let it go. You know, I remember when I was graduating high school I was afraid. It was like I was entering the real world. I thought she was feeling that, or it had to do with a boy."

"John Wheeler?"

"Could have been. I know she liked John, but I knew she wouldn't end up with him."

"Why did you have that feeling?"

She shrugged. "Some of it was a mother's intuition, but I heard her on the phone with somebody who wasn't John."

"Do you have a name?"

"Sorry, I don't."

"Okay. Anything else that night?"

"Nothing unusual. Brian went to bed at nine, and we watched the *X-Files* together." She smiled. "Debbie always liked David Duchovny. Then she went to her room, and I read for about an hour before washing up."

"Did she get any phone calls or visitors?"

"No. There really was nothing unusual that night."

"Tell me about the next day."

"I was up before the kids, about seven. I heard Debbie in the bathroom. She sounded like she was throwing up. I went to check on her, but she said she was okay. She came out looking pale. I felt her forehead, but it was cool."

"Did she throw up?"

"She said no. I'm pretty sure she did, but I learned not to press a teenage daughter, especially in the morning." She laughed.

"Did she eat breakfast?"

"She wasn't big on breakfast. I think she nibbled on a piece of toast that morning. Why?"

"Just trying to recreate events. It helps your recall when you remember minute details. After breakfast, what happened?"

"She left for school, and I had taken the day off to get my hair and nails done."

"What time did Debbie get home from school?"

"It was a half a day for them. School was just about over then. She came home around twelve thirty."

"Were you home?"

"Yes, my hair appointment was at one, and Debbie looked after Brian when I went."

"Did she stay home or go out?"

"She had a friend, Angela, over."

"What time did you get back?"

"After the hair salon, I went for a manicure and got home around four."

The time women put into looking good was amazing. "Was her friend Angela still there?"

"Yes. They were hanging out by the pool."

"Did Debbie stay home until you left for the wedding?"

"Yes. Her friend left sometime around five."

"And no one came over before you left?"

"No. When I left, Debbie and Brian were the only people here."

I closed my notebook and took the tiniest sip of coffee. "Did Debbie know an Igor Papadakis?"

"Papadakis? No, not that I know of."

I fished a picture of a younger Papadakis out of my pocket. She studied it before shaking her head. "No."

"Did Debbie have any blond-haired girlfriends that she had a recent disagreement with?"

She smiled. "This is Florida. We have a lot of blonds. But not that I can think of. Why?"

"There was a report that a blond female was sighted at the park that night."

She jumped up. "Let's go up to her room. We can look at her yearbooks."

As I followed her down the hall, she stopped and said, "That man, in the picture. He had blond hair on the long side. Do you think it could be him?"

All the sleepless nights this poor woman had endured had turned her into an amateur sleuth.

"We're looking into every possibility, no matter how remote."

The room was as bright and unsettling as the first time I saw it.

"It's okay, come on in."

Axel Rose scowled at me from the Guns N' Roses poster as I stepped in. Mrs. Boyle went to the nightstand and pulled open a drawer. "Here's her yearbook." She gently ran her hand over it. "Last year's is in the closet."

"Last year's?"

"They started doing junior yearbooks as well. I thought it was crazy then, but I'm glad to have it now."

I circled the room, studying as I went along. It was a typical female teenager's room—lots of girlie things and childhood mementos. There was a turtle on the boom box that she'd probably painted back in grammar school. It reminded me of a stingray ashtray I'd made when I was a similar age.

I took the shell off the turtle. "I'm not being nosy, but who does this belong to?"

"Oh yeah, I remember that."

It was ring, a college graduation ring from Rutgers University in New Jersey. It was stamped with the year 1984.

"Is it her father's?"

"No, Peter went to Louisiana State."

"Any idea who it might belong to?"

"I'd forgotten about it. Nineteen eighty-four? That makes whoever owned it around fifty-five today. Let me think it over. If anything comes to mind, I'll let you know."

"Great. In the meantime, can I ask you to leave it in Mr. Turtle and not touch it?"

"Oh my God. You think it's a clue?"

"I don't know anything more than it's an old college ring. For all I know, she could have found it when she was twelve and forgotten about it. It's probably nothing but a one in a zillion chance, but I'd like it as uncontaminated as possible."

"You're right."

I put the turtle's shell back on.

Mrs. Boyle said, "Here are the yearbooks. You want to go through them?"

I thumbed opened to a page of portraits and saw all the notes made by students under their pictures. Who knew what I could find reading them? "I—I don't have the time right now, but if you don't mind, I'd like to borrow them for a while. I promise to be careful with them."

She hesitated before agreeing. I asked her about what classes Debbie had taken her last year and was shocked when Mrs. Boyle rattled each of the subjects and the teachers' names. Asking her to repeat them, I jotted down the names and wrapped up my visit.

Chapter 27

I was sitting behind my desk, taking another departmental survey, when Derrick swung into the office.

"Wheeler's wife said both of his parents died of cancer, and his doctor said to avoid radiation if he could."

What about the sun? Wheeler didn't have a tan, but most people who lived here didn't. It was only the tourists and part-timers who couldn't get enough rays.

"No surprise. I'll bet Wheeler told his wife, and she's covering for him."

"She couldn't make up both his parents getting cancer. Besides, she said Wheeler had an MRI about fifteen years ago."

"He did?"

"She said Wheeler was working on a ladder and took a fall. He banged his head and was taken to the hospital."

"Where'd they take him?"

"NCH Baker, downtown."

I got up. "Let's go."

"Hold on. I called them, and they have to retrieve the records from storage."

"It's not digital?"

"No, that was in 2003, before they started storing everything in the cloud."

"How long until they dig it out?"

"They said it wouldn't be till after the holidays. They keep them off-site at a temperature-controlled storage place, and it closes between Christmas and New Year's."

"But Christmas isn't till next week."

"I'll call them again, but that's what they told me."

"Tell them it's urgent."

"I did."

"Tell them again. Look, I gotta run out and pick something up."

Talking about Christmas reminded me I had to get something to put under the tree for Mary Ann. My big gift was the trip. But that was for both of us, even though it was for her. I had to get another thing or two for her.

Mary Ann being into yoga, and Lululemon having a sale made it easy. I circled Waterside Shops' parking lot twice before sticking the police sticker on the dashboard. The mall was jammed with shoppers, most holding two bags or more. How much did this place do on a day like today?

Passing De Beers Jewelers I saw a couple entering the store. I froze. Was it one of the handbag couples? Pretending to look at De Beers window display, I saw the couple being helped at a counter. I surveyed the interior of the shop and my heart raced. At the back counter was another familiar couple.

The male had on the same blue sport jacket and designer sunglasses one of the bag thieves wore. Was this gang elevating their game? I checked the reflections in the window for any accomplices who might be spotting for them.

Over my right shoulder was a suspicious-looking man holding up a newspaper but not reading it. I shifted my attention to the first couple and my stomach dropped. The male was slipping a piece of jewelry into his jacket.

Approaching the entrance, a De Beers salesman opened the door for me. I stepped in, pulled the door closed, and slapped handcuffs on its handles. I drew my gun and shouted, "Put your hands in the air. It's the police."

* * *

Derrick shoved the *Naples Daily News* into his drawer as I entered the office. I said, "It's okay, I saw it."

"You all right?"

Even though my stomach burned, I said, "Yeah, don't worry about me."

"You sure? I heard the sheriff is pissed."

"I know. I'm heading up there now."

"Good luck."

I remembered the same feeling when I was summoned to the principal's office in fifth grade. I thought I was going to be suspended for punching a classmate who'd embarrassed me in front of a girl I had a crush on. This time the circumstances were more serious.

Chester didn't get up or offer his hand. He threw a chin toward a chair. I eased myself down, keeping my eyes off the pile of newspapers on the corner of his desk. Chester put an elbow on the arm of his chair and placed his other hand on his hip.

"Where should we start, Detective?"

I hated it when he addressed me like that. I understood it in a formal setting, but we'd worked together for over a year, and I'd caught the serial killer when he was doubting my ability.

"I'm sorry. It was an honest mistake. I was certain they were with the handbag ring."

"The mistaken identity is excusable, but you're a damn cowboy, Luca. You broke every rule, endangering not only yourself but scores of holiday shoppers. You should have called for a backup. You could have quietly questioned them. But no, you handcuff the doors and draw your gun?"

"I—"

"I'm not finished. Instead of everyone talking about the Christmas Parade last night, they're talking about this department and its rogue officers. It's not even nine o'clock, but I've been getting reamed by the mayor, town councilmen, and Waterside's management. And there's two messages from the Collier family's attorney. Of all the people in the world, you had to pick on the Collier family. What in the name of God were you thinking?"

"Both couples resembled the bag crew—same clothes and the sunglasses. They kept them on, and they were the same glitzy ones they had on in Saks. I observed them, and when I saw the male pocket a ring, I just sprang into action."

"It was his mother's ring, for Chrissakes! He wanted De Beers to copy it. Even if he was stealing, you know a place like that has more cameras than the county jail. If De Beers confirmed missing a ring, you could have asked him to produce what he pocketed. If he refused, you could have used the store's video."

"I understand, sir. I guess I was a little too anxious to put an end to this gang."

He shook his head.

"A little anxious? You broke every protocol in the book."

"It won't happen again, sir."

"I should be putting you on administrative leave. I think you deserve to be, but you're lucky, I don't feel like dealing with the union."

Staring at my feet as I left Chester's office, I felt so low that I could have played handball against the curb. If Derrick started asking me questions about what Chester said I'd lose it. I took the back stairs and headed to the parking lot. Since my mother was long gone, I called Mary Ann.

Chapter 28

The FBI report on Igor Papadakis was really just a summary. Igor Papadakis was born on November 13, 1965, in a suburb of St. Petersburg called Dubrovka, to George and Natasha Papadakis. He had no siblings. At fifteen, he'd been arrested during a student protest over the food quality at the high school.

The family moved to Greece on December 20, 1985, when Igor was twenty. They settled in Papagou, just outside of Athens.

In April of 1987, Igor Papadakis was questioned by the Hellenic Police about the murder of Spiro Xeanax, a sixteen-year-old male from Aryiroupolis.

Two witnesses had placed Igor Papadakis near the scene of the murder. Papadakis denied any knowledge of the killing, claiming he was out talking a walk. The Hellenic Police noted that Papadakis lived more than ten miles away and had no business in the area.

The Hellenic Police notified Interpol about their interest in making sure he did not leave the country. They also seized his passport. There were two other suspects in the case, one a known pedophile.

In April of 1989, the investigation was terminated and Papadakis was given back his passport but advised to notify the authorities about any international travel. In May of 1989, Igor Papadakis left Greece without telling the authorities.

The death of Spiro Xeanax remains unsolved.

I reread it. What jumped out at me was the timing. They moved out of Russia just days before Christmas? Then Papadakis is in Greece just over a year and he's questioned for murder? Was it an immigrant being targeted? Was trouble following Papadakis, or was he bringing it with him?

Could the family have fled Russia in a hurry because their son got in trouble? We weren't on the best of terms with the Russians these days, and it was thirty years ago. Would they be willing to check into Papadakis? That was during the KGB days. They probably knew when you sneezed.

Leaning back in my chair, I remembered Papadakis saying he lived in Miami when he first came to the States. Was that even true? I'd have Derrick do a search for all his known addresses and then check the areas against any unsolved murders.

As I considered other avenues to pursue, I stared at the yearbooks on the corner of my desk and grabbed one. It was from 1993, the year Debbie Boyle was supposed to graduate high school.

I flipped through, looking for her class. It was on the third page of the Class of 1993 section. Five rows, five pictures each, of kids posing stared at me. All the kids except one had neon smiles on.

Some of the kids had left handwritten messages under their photos. Good luck wishes dominated, with remember this or that, but there were two that stood out. One was from a girl named Donna Siler: "Don't worry, it will work out. I'll be there for you."

The other was under Debbie Boyle's picture: "You're going to regret it." It was signed Fred. Who was Fred, and what did he mean with his message? I went to the beginning of the book and went page by page looking for a boy named Fred.

The first couple of pages were the administrative staff and teachers. Then a couple of pages of the school's band and theater groups in action before the class pictures. I found the first Fred. A shaggy-haired kid named Fredrick Holmes. He was a junior. I jotted it down and continued searching. The second, a senior, was a kid with a crooked smile named Fred Biehl.

As I went page by page, I came to a two-page spread of pictures from a Halloween party. There was no missing Debbie Boyle in her short-skirted maid's outfit. A blond-haired man had his arms around her shoulder. He looked familiar. I went to the pages of teacher's pictures. His hair wasn't long, but there was no doubt it was Larry Culver.

He was the teacher involved in the SAT test scandal. Maybe I should have a chat with him. The last Fred I found went by the name

Freddy Palmer. He had thick-framed glasses and hair that looked electrified.

* * *

"Since you had a feeling about Papadakis from day one, I thought you'd like to follow up on a new angle with him."

I swore his ears perked up like a hunting dog. "Sure. What's going on?"

"Something in the FBI report started me thinking. The entire family left Russia days before Christmas. Does that sound right to you? Who would move at that time of the year?"

"Unless you had to."

"Exactly. Maybe Igor got in trouble and they took off."

"You want me to see what the Russians have on him?"

"Yeah, but also and probably more troubling is the fact that the kid in Greece was murdered about a year after Papadakis moved there. When he took off for America he told us he went to Miami."

"Yeah, I remember that."

"But did he? Check all known addresses for him. Then run a cross-check, say fifty miles of any address, against any unsolved murders."

Derrick nodded. "Damn good idea, Frank."

"We'll see about that."

"Say, why don't we ask that FBI friend of yours for help with the Russians?"

"Let's hold off. I don't want to abuse the relationship. Save it for when we really need something."

Chapter 29

Pissed over wasting half the day in court, I was peeling my jacket off when Derrick said, "Frank, I went through the Boyle evidence box, and guess what I found?"

I hated when people said that. "This isn't a game, Derrick."

"Sorry. There was a fingernail collected from the scene. It was Debbie Boyle's for sure, same nail polish."

"What? It wasn't cataloged?"

"Nope. Whoever handled the evidence stuffed it in the pocket of Boyle's jeans. You think we can get DNA off it?"

"Let's hope she fought, scratching her murderer, and there's some skin there."

"That's what I was hoping."

"We have to get it to the lab. Fast. Who knows what will turn up."

"Even if it's twenty-five years old they can still tell who it belongs to, right?"

"Yeah, DNA lasts a couple of million years. Were there any other surprises in the box?"

"No. It was moldy, but I went through everything completely."

It was what I should have done, would have done more thoroughly, before chemo brain. "Get the nail over to the lab. I'll tell them it's coming."

This was the break we were working for. It wasn't really a break but a discovery that Detective Foster and his team had made another blunder. Foster didn't have homicide experience and deserved some slack, but failing to simply catalog items collected from a crime scene bordered on negligence.

I wondered if we'd get a tell from any of the suspects when we asked them for DNA samples. Wheeler and Papadakis were fighting for pole position as far as leading suspects were concerned, and I could see both of them making a fuss, refusing to submit samples.

What Mackay's reaction would be was a wild card I couldn't call. I didn't think it was Walker, but we needed a sample to be sure.

Sleazebag Boralis would be analyzed as well. I'd even make sure Bert Campos be tested, but other than finding out the old hippy was missing a chromosome or two, I didn't expect to discover anything. And there was Moore, who had threatened her. Would his DNA match?

* * *

Derrick came in looking like a kid who'd had his bike taken away from him. "The lab said it'd be at least a week if not ten days until they could examine the nail fragment."

"I know. When I called they said Miller was on vacation until after the New Year. He went skiing out west somewhere."

"So now we got to wait on it."

"I called Peters, see if he could do anything to speed it up, but he gave me the bullshit about it being a twenty-five-year-old case and another couple of weeks wouldn't matter."

"How come you never moved upstairs?"

"You mean going for promotions?"

"Yeah, you have what it takes to run this place, if you ask me."

I snorted. "No way. I don't have the people skills. The upper crust here must be political and politically correct. I'm about as far from that as you can get."

"But why not a lieutenant or captain? Or at least a sarge. You deserve it, plus the pay is better."

"I do what I do because I love it. I'm not saying it isn't depressing or even revolting at times, but getting into the mind of a killer and tracking 'em down is very satisfying. I couldn't imagine doing anything else, especially some political desk job."

"But you could get promoted to sarge and still get into the field."

"I'm good at what I do and want to focus on it full time, not worry about paperwork."

"How long you planning on staying a homicide detective?"

"Until they kick me out or I drop dead." It wasn't totally true, because if my memory kept declining I'd want to leave before they booted me out.

"I love the fact that you're all-in, Frank. I got lucky with you. I'm getting trained by the best."

If he thinks I'm the best now, he should have seen me before I got bladder cancer. Or better yet, he should have seen me when JJ was my partner up in Jersey. I smiled at the thought of how good we were.

"What are you smiling about?"

"Just reminiscing about the old days and my partner JJ. We solved a ton of cases, and there were a lot of tough ones."

"This is a pretty tough one, isn't it?"

"Medium, but we're inches away from solving it."

Chapter 30

This would be our first Christmas living together. It wasn't quite the feeling a ten-year-old gets, but there was a certain electricity in the air, and it helped bury my embarrassment over the De Beers screwup.

I even violated one of my rules and got a real tree. The pine smell in the house was a nice touch, but the needles were dropping in a steady drizzle. If I ever got another live tree, I'd be sure to get it earlier.

It was also the first Christmas since things went south with my ex-wife that my melancholia stayed below the surface. I was excited about surprising Mary Ann with the European trip and looked forward to some quiet time alone.

Neither of us had any close family, either in relationship or in geography, and for Christmas Eve we were going to a friend of Mary Ann's who lived in the community.

"What is Becky making tomorrow? Fish?"

"No, she said it was going to be Southern styled, with a ham and prime rib."

I grew up in an Italian family where the Feast of the Seven Fishes defined dinner on Christmas Eve. Protecting my heritage and arteries, I said, "I'll go to the Captain and Krewe Seafood Market in the morning and pick up some fish for Christmas Day."

"Sounds good. What are you in the mood for?"

"I'll get some lobster tails and shrimp and a piece of fish, maybe grouper."

"Sounds like a lot."

"You should have seen Christmas when my mother was alive. At least seven different fish. We're only gonna have three."

"I'll get some smoked salmon as an appetizer."

"Now we're talking. That gets us to four, more than halfway there.

Not bad, considering there's only two of us."

"You're a piece of work, Frank."

"It's our first Christmas. We got to do it right."

Mary Ann pecked my cheek. "Sometimes you can really be sweet."

"I've been thinking. It's important that we start making our own traditions together."

"You're right. We should."

Even though I had drifted from attending church, I said, "Why don't we go to Midnight Mass on Christmas Eve, after dinner?"

"That would be nice, a special way to celebrate Christmas together. I never went to Midnight Mass."

"We used to go every year, and when we got home my mom would make a batch of fresh zeppole."

"We'll go to church, but I'm not making pastries at one o'clock in the morning."

"That's a deal. By the way, there's no gift opening on Christmas Eve."

Mary Ann put a pout on. "Even after Mass? It's officially Christmas then."

"You can open just one."

* * *

Christmas Eve was a little weird. Her friend Becky had her family over as well, making me feel like an outsider. The food was so-so, but Mass was magical. I insisted on going to Saint Williams, figuring most of the old-timers who crowded the place would be sleeping. Plus, they had an awesome musical program with a dozen instruments and a large choir.

Saint Williams was full but not packed. You could feel the joy in the room. We sang along to Christmas carols and stayed to the very end. When we got home, I turned our tree lights on and it looked amazing. We admired it for twenty minutes before crawling into bed. It was after two.

The next morning, I woke up just before nine. Mary Ann was in a deep sleep. After trying to stay in bed, I slid out and made coffee. I opened the sliders and sat on the lanai. I had to get my sunglasses. It was in the low seventies and quiet.

Having a second cup, I turned the tree on. At ten fifteen I put Christmas music on, but still no Mary Ann. Ten minutes passed before I raised the volume. "The Christmas Song" was playing when Mary Ann came into the room.

Wearing a smile that lit up the room, and a silky, blue camisole that lit up little Luca, she said, "Merry Christmas, Frank." I gave her a kiss and a coffee, and we exchanged gifts. She liked the Lululemon outfits, even though I screwed up the sizes. She was excited over the European vacation, but I got the feeling she knew about the trip.

We lingered around, took a shower together and hopped in bed for a lovefest. It was my kind of Christmas.

We lounged around the rest of the afternoon making a couple of holiday calls. For dinner, we did it Florida style, grilling seafood and sipping wine al fresco. It was the best Christmas I'd had in decades.

I was never a fan of New Year's and the nonsense about making resolutions to change this or do that. If you wanted to quit smoking, get in shape, or go bungee jumping, why did you have to wait for New Year's to commit to it? Every day was a new day, a new start, and an opportunity to live the life you wanted. Why waste a damn year?

New Year's was amateur night, in my opinion, and it's not a humble one either. I stopped going out before I went into the academy. My idea of a good New Year's Eve was a small house party with good food and wine. It took a bit of convincing, but coming on the heels of such a good Christmas together, I was able to convince Mary Ann to go to an early dinner at Bleu Provence.

We had a nice time, but driving home my mind shifted to the Boyle case and the pending DNA and MRI results.

I took every case as a personal challenge. It was me against the killer. We were locked in a battle that I needed to win. I knew it was my job and the community benefitted, but I also knew, deep down, that I needed the confirmation and respect that came along with it.

This case was different. I wanted the win, but I also wanted the win for the victim's mother. The poor woman had suffered far too long. A solve here wouldn't bring her daughter back, but it might help her move on with the rest of her life.

I was betting the house that the next couple of days would provide the clues we'd need to solve this ice-cold case.

Chapter 31

"How was New Year's, Frank?"

"Nice and quiet. How about you?"

"We went to my parents. Nothing big. We were home just after midnight."

"Mary Ann made me stay up and watch the ball drop. Why is that such a big deal? It doesn't mean a thing."

"Can't imagine those people standing out there for hours, freezing their butts off."

"Amen. Look, we're going to get the DNA results any day now, and I want to be ready to cross-check them."

"Okay. What do you want to do?"

"Let's get out to all suspects and see if they'll submit to a DNA test voluntarily."

"But we don't even know if there is any DNA on the fingernail."

"I'm aware of that. But I'm believing there will be."

"But if there is, it could be female."

"Look, I make the plans here. Okay? We're going to learn something about each of the suspects. See how they react to the request; it's intel we can use. Plus, we'll have DNA samples for anyone who agrees to be tested. That's a good thing."

"Okay. I see. Just so you know, Frank, I wasn't challenging. I was just asking questions, that's all."

I looked in his face. He was lying. "Let's move on. I want you to go and see Mackay, Campos, and Boralis. You've got to pay attention to how they react. Notice everything they say and do. Body language will tell you a lot. You got that? Pick up a couple of swab kits from the lab and be careful. Use gloves."

Derrick nodded. "I understand, but why Campos? He's not the one who did it."

"We both believe he didn't, but he was there at Delnor that night. We've got to know for certain. If he's not a match, we scratch him off the list."

"I guess that's the way it should be handled."

"You seem to be questioning me today. I hope you don't make it a habit."

"No, no, I wasn't. It's just that it seems like a waste of time, considering we have more credible suspects like Papadakis, Wheeler, Walker, and Moore to run down."

"I'm going to see them. When you get done with them, call me. Maybe we can meet up."

My original plan was to do all the visits together. I didn't need help, but Derrick needed the experience. A seasoned detective could glean a ton of information by the way people reacted. But Derrick had pissed me off, questioning me on the DNA. He needed to do a little grunt work to get back into my good graces.

I told myself it wasn't revenge. The lesser suspects had to be visited, and it would be wasting my time if I did it and negligent if we omitted them. I lingered around, making a couple of calls before heading out. That way, Derrick would be sure to meet me in time to visit a suspect or two.

It was my third visit with John Wheeler. He was working on a commercial job site in Venetian Village and agreed to meet. I didn't want to raise any suspicions and wanted to keep the issue private. He was working on the south-end side of Venetian Village, a development of stores and restaurants on two bay-front parcels straddling Park Shore Drive.

The views and the vibe of Venetian Village were great, especially off-season, as it tended to get touristy. Putting my sunglasses on, I settled onto a bench by a jumping water fountain. Ice cream cones in hand, a father and son were coming out of Ben and Jerry's as I spotted Wheeler.

I stuck up a hand, and Wheeler nodded in acknowledgment. He was wearing a long-sleeved safari shirt, jeans, and a floppy hat, protection from the sun when working outdoors.

He stuck his hand out as he approached, and I stood and shook it. I never liked a man who wouldn't get up to shake hands.

"Thanks for meeting me, Mr. Wheeler."

"No problem. I appreciate the discretion you showed. Everyone knows the case has been reopened, and I've had a lot of questions about it. What's up?"

"We'd like to ask you to voluntarily submit a DNA sample."

"A DNA sample? Why?"

"It's routine."

"Routine? Come on, Detective. What's going on?"

"We believe we've been able to recover DNA from the crime scene."

"The crime scene? It happened over twenty-five years ago."

"Let me rephrase that. A piece of evidence that was recovered at the crime scene at the time was just discovered."

"What do you mean by just discovered?"

"It was never cataloged and was stuffed in a pocket of Debbie's jeans. I can't answer why, and you didn't hear it from me, but it's another example of how poorly this case was handled."

"Sounds fishy to me. The police plant evidence all the time."

I knew it was going to be a credibility issue. It should be, and if it turned out to be a critically incriminating piece of evidence, it would be attacked in court by defense attorneys.

"I'm not in a position to say that never happens, but it is a very rare occurrence. The only people who have had access to the evidence in this case are me and my partner. I can assure you we have not tampered with it."

"I'm uncomfortable with this whole thing. First, you want me to get an MRI, and now to submit to some DNA test. For some reason, you're gunning for me. I don't get it."

"If I'm gunning for anything, it's the truth. That's all. A long time ago, when I first started out in homicide, I was involved in a case where the wrong man was arrested. Since that time, I've worked like hell to make sure it never happens on any case I'm working."

"It's not like I don't trust you, but why should I? What good would it do me?"

"It would clear you beyond doubt, erase any suspicions people may have."

"Look, until you came along, nobody had talked about this case for years. I'm sorry. I'm not willing to go through with this."

Wheeler made the right argument and seemed genuine about it. But on the other side, he now refused two tests to clarify his role. Did we need to elevate him? Since the old MRI of his would be available later today or tomorrow it made no sense to waste any energy on him now.

* * *

When I called Clem Walker, he agreed to meet me but down at the Naples City Dock. Why would someone who claimed to fish off the beach be at a marina?

There was a briny smell in the air as I waited at the entrance, as Walker instructed. I watched a steady stream of people coming in from an afternoon on the water. A minibus pulled up, discharging a group of businessmen who asked for directions to a catamaran named *Sweet Liberty*. I pointed out where it was docked, and as they told me about the cocktail cruise they were taking, I saw Walker walking in the parking lot.

Walker had a T-shirt with a sailfish on it, flip-flops, and dungaree cutoffs. He put his cigarette in his mouth and stuck his hand out.

"How you doing?"

"Good. You been out fishing?"

"Nah, met some friends for lunch at the Dock." He hiked a thumb over his shoulder. The Dock was a busy place, perched on the marina's edge, that catered to the fishing set and tourists.

"Haven't been there in a long while." It had great views but was loud and didn't take reservations.

"What did you want to talk about?"

"Would you voluntarily submit to a DNA test?"

He took a long pull on his cigarette. "As long as it's on the up-and-up."

"Absolutely."

"I'd like to know what this is all about."

I told him about the newly found evidence.

"I got nothing to worry about, so let's get it over with."

"Why don't we go to my car?"

Once in the car, Walker signed the consent form and I opened the kit. I pulled on latex gloves and cracked open the glass storage tube to make it easier to slip in the samples after collection.

Walker opened his mouth, revealing a set of nicotine-stained teeth. I swabbed the inside of his cheek with the Q-tip, ejected the tip into the tube, and repeated the process with the other side of his cheek.

Walker was an enigma. Parts of his story didn't fit, but neither did any of the others. He didn't flinch at giving up a sample, but with a twenty-five-year-old case the attorneys would battle it out if it came to it. As I pulled out of the parking lot, Derrick called.

Chapter 32

Sitting in Coastland Mall's parking lot and talking to Mary Ann, I saw Derrick pull in. He gave me a big wave and an even bigger smile. Was he trying to get back in my good graces or just excited about interviewing with me?

He climbed into the Cherokee, and before the door was shut, said, "I went three for three. How'd you make out?"

"You got DNA samples from Mackay, Boralis, and Campos?"

"Yep. I have to be honest with you, it was easy."

Didn't people realize how stupid it sounded to say they were being honest? "Mackay didn't put up a fuss?"

"Not really. He was skeptical. Boralis gave me some bullshit that he hoped we weren't going to frame him. I mean, do people really think the police are that corrupt?"

"That's the billion-dollar question. We had some issues up in Jersey, as I'm sure you did in DC. The way I see it, the larger the force, the more opportunities there are for corruption."

"You're probably right. How'd you do?"

"Wheeler wouldn't go for it. He was worried that the new evidence was planted. But Walker had no problem with it."

"You think Wheeler was scared?"

"Hard to say. He's cooperated to a degree, but I say table it until we get the MRI."

"Makes sense. Who we seeing?"

"We only have to see Papadakis. I didn't want to drive up to Sarasota for nothing, so I called Moore. He agreed to give a sample but wanted it done under supervision. I arranged for him to give a sample to the Sarasota Police."

"Another one who thinks he'd be framed?"

"I guess with a case this old, it makes people suspicious. Anyway, call NCH and see where the hell that MRI is."

By the time we pulled up to Papadakis's green house, NCH had confirmed the MRI was ready, and Derrick had sent a text to have it picked up and sent to Dr. Brown, a radiologist we worked with.

The dog was barking, but unlike the last time, wasn't chained to a stake. I told Derrick to knock on the door. The garage door was open, and I wanted to have a look.

My eyes teared from a strong smell of bleach. What was he disinfecting or eliminating? I peered inside. Black plastic bags were piled under and on top of a wooden workbench. On the opposite side was a rusty lawn mower, two shovels, a tool box, and a padlocked wooden chest. Derrick called my name, and I trotted over to the front door.

Papadakis was neatly dressed in beige chinos and a blue golf shirt. He must have washed his hair; his coal-colored strands were fluffy. Papadakis grabbed the collar of his barking dog.

"Good to see both of you again."

"Could you lock the dog up?"

"Gorky's not dangerous. But if you want, I'll tie him up."

"Please."

We stepped aside and Papadakis led the dog to the stake and chained him to it. Then he looked over his shoulder at us and closed the garage door.

"Thanks."

"Gorky's a good boy. He just needs to know you."

"I couldn't help but notice your garage."

"It's a little messy."

"That chest. It looks European. Did you take it over when you came?"

"Yes. It belonged to my father."

"You have it locked up pretty tight."

He shrugged. "Why don't you come in?"

"You have anything particular in the chest?"

"Just some personal family stuff, you know."

We went back to the kitchen, which was noticeably brighter this time. I scanned the countertops—nothing.

"Sit, sit."

We sat, but Papadakis stood.

"What did you want to see me about?"

"We'd like to ask you to submit a DNA sample."

His lip quivered. "A DNA sample? What for?"

"To check against the DNA collected at the Boyle crime scene."

"But that was so long ago."

Derrick slid a kit onto the kitchen table. "It doesn't matter."

When Papadakis shifted on his feet, for a split second I thought he was going to run.

"I don't have to do it, right?"

I said, "It's voluntary, but if you have nothing to hide, you shouldn't be afraid of giving us a sample."

"I don't know. Someone could take my DNA and put it somewhere to get me in trouble."

I was tired of the framing excuse. "I don't believe that's a valid fear. Are you insinuating that the police could plant your DNA and frame you?"

"I've seen it happen."

"Well, first off, we don't do that, and I've never been part of any force that was accused of that. But more importantly, if someone wanted to do that, including the police, your DNA is all over—your hairbrush, your toothbrush, your clothing—it's all over."

"So why do you need me to take a test?"

"We don't really need to."

"What? I—I—How does that work? I mean, you can take my DNA from anywhere?"

"We leave our DNA all over the things we touch, like the steering wheel of your car."

Papadakis's pasty face turned flour white. He said, "I gotta go to the bathroom." And he disappeared down the hallway.

Derrick flashed a thumbs-up and extended his fist for a bump. Fist bumping? Where did this start?

I whispered, "Keep it in check."

There was a flush of a toilet and Papadakis reappeared. "Sorry. When I gotta go, I really have to go."

"No problem, I understand." And I did. "Are you going to agree to a test?"

He wagged his head. "I don't think so. I think it would be a good idea if I consulted with an attorney."

As we pulled away, Derrick said, "That was awesome. He fell apart when you told him about getting his DNA without a test."

"He's hiding something. What the hell was in that chest?"

"We could get a subpoena."

"No judge would sign off on it; we don't have enough."

"Yet. We get his DNA, we'll send it to Greece, see if he's connected to that boy's murder. And Russia. Who knows what they'll find?"

"One step at a time. We don't work for Interpol."

"I know, but even if he's not Boyle's killer, he could still be the one who killed that Greek boy. Or somebody else."

It was a strong point that I'd missed and shouldn't have. "Maybe."

Chapter 33

The lunchroom was crowded. Phil Murray was retiring. Phil was a quiet patrolman who didn't like attention, otherwise we'd be saying goodbye at the Old Naples Pub in Venetian Village. Instead, it was wraps, deli sandwiches, and soda, rather than beer and burgers.

Halfway through a turkey wrap, Barbara, a public relations officer, tapped my shoulder.

"This just came in for you."

It was a large manila envelope from Dr. Brown. It was the MRI. I shoved the balance of my wrap in my mouth on the way to my office.

I waved the envelope. "We got the MRI results."

Derrick popped out of his seat as I tore open the envelope. "And the winner is!"

A two-page report and DVD fell out of the envelope. I scanned Dr. Brown's report. It was packed with medical jargon. I flipped to the second-page summary.

The highlights were:

Evidence of an old fracture to the frontal bone that has healed.

Origin - Likely caused by blunt force trauma.

Derrick said, "He did have a fracture. I guess he was hit that night."

"No way to prove if the fracture happened that night or some other time in his life prior to that night."

"You think so?"

"It doesn't matter, we have the DNA results coming in. Fracture or not, if his DNA is under her fingernail, Wheeler is our guy."

"But we don't have his DNA to compare with."

"We get the results, see if it's a match for anyone in the database and the ones we collected. If there's no match, I'll get us some of his DNA."

***

Mary Ann was folding laundry when I came in. She said, "What's the matter?"

"Nothing."

She put down a towel. "Don't tell me nothing."

"I'm telling you, it's nothing."

"Frank, if you want to walk around holding in whatever is bothering you, be my guest, but don't ruin my night by brooding around."

She was right again. "I'm just a little pissed, that's all."

"About?"

"The Wheeler MRI came in. There was evidence of an old fracture."

"So?"

"He was a main suspect."

"Okay, so now he's not. Like you always told me, eliminating a suspect is good, it focuses things."

I hated it when she threw back what I'd said. I needed a little sympathy. "Let's hope so."

Mary Ann came over and wrapped her arms around me. "Poor little Frankie is disappointed." She tickled my armpit.

"Hey, no fair." I pinned her arms and kissed her.

She wrapped one of her legs around mine and ground her hips into me. I picked her up and carried her to the bedroom for the ultimate consolation.

***

Derrick answered the phone. "Frank, it's Dempsey, from forensics."

I grabbed the phone. "Rick, it's Frank. What do you have for me?"

"We profiled the skin cells on the fingernail and ran a cross-check on the database, but no cold hits."

"What about the swab samples we gave you? Did you check it against them?"

"First thing we did, Frank."

"Are you sure?"

"I'm sorry, Frank. There's no match."

"Did you run it through the national data bank?"

"Yes, and Florida's as well, but no hits."

"I'm coming down."

"I don't have the time, Frank. There's no match, and you coming is not going to change it."

"All right. Thanks, Rick. There's two other people of interest that refused to submit samples. I'm going to collect specimens and get them to you."

"No problem. You get them, and we'll run a check. I gotta run."

"Hold on, was the DNA male or female?"

"Male."

"Thanks."

I slammed the phone down. "We can't seem to catch a break in this case. The only thing we found out is it's male."

"We've still got Wheeler and Papadakis to check."

"I know."

"You know, you can't forget that whatever was on the victim's fingernail didn't have to be her killer's."

"Of course. It's just that I've got a feeling about it."

"That's good enough for me. What do you want to do?"

"Find out when the recycling truck picks up from Wheeler's neighborhood."

"Recycling?"

"Yeah. Wheeler's a root beer drinker. Go to his house the morning the truck goes and grab three empty cans out of his trash."

Derrick looked at me like I'd kicked his dog.

"That's right, this is the real world, not *CSI*."

We both reached for our phones. I called Papadakis and made an appointment to see him again.

The recycling truck was coming to Wheeler's neighborhood in the morning. I reminded Derrick to wear gloves, to bag the cans separately, and left to see Papadakis.

* * *

The dog was chained, guarding the property and barking, as I walked to the door. Papadakis's garage was closed. It hit me that the chain wasn't long enough to prevent an intruder from reaching the front door. I pictured the padlocked trunk sitting in the garage and rang the bell.

The door swung open before the sound of the bell disappeared. There was a tiny bead of sweat running down the side of Papadakis's face.

"Detective Luca, come in."

"Does that dog ever stop barking?"

"Gorky! Calm down!" He followed me into the hallway. "He's a good dog, really good."

In the kitchen I asked, "Can I have a bottle of water?"

"Sure." He swung the refrigerator open and took one bottle out. Swapping bottles was out.

"Have you reconsidered allowing us to take a swab for DNA?"

He sat on a kitchen chair. "Uh, no, I mean. I don't think so."

"Okay."

"There's really no reason that I should."

"It would help eliminate you as a suspect in the Boyle murder."

"But—I didn't do anything. I was just walking—"

"Like you were in Ariypool, where that kid Spiro was found dead?"

Papadakis's shoulders sagged. "It was Aryiroupolis, and I had nothing to do with that boy's death. They tried to frame me. We'd just moved to Greece, and a kid is killed, and they think I did it. The Greeks don't like Russians. Even though my father was Greek, they treated us like second-class people."

"Is that why you ran as soon as you had your passport back?"

"The way we were treated over that boy's death was disgusting. How could anyone stay there?"

"But you left alone. If it was so bad, why did your parents stay behind?"

His face crumpled, and he hung his head. Was he going to confess?

"My mama, she was sick with cancer. She couldn't travel. I never saw her again."

He seemed genuinely upset. Still, I'm sure there have been thousands of killers who've lost their mother to cancer.

"I'm sorry to hear that. Do you mind if I use your bathroom?"

"Of course not. It's the second door on the right."

It was past my time to take a leak, but the fifteen minutes it would take to coax one out would raise suspicions.

I wanted to take his toothbrush, but he'd know what I was doing and might run again. I looked in the waste can. There were two Plackers he'd used to clean his teeth. Gross, but a good source of DNA. I pulled on gloves and bagged the floss tools. Sliding the tub door, I spied two dark hairs by the drain and bagged them as well.

I flushed the toilet, ran the sink for a minute, and came out wiping my hands on my pants.

"Thanks."

"No problem."

"So, tell me. You left Russia in 1985."

"Yes. It was difficult with communism falling: a good thing, but chaotic, so we left for Greece."

"You left in a hurry."

He hesitated. "No, I don't think so."

"You left just days before Christmas. That seems unusual to me."

"Were we anxious to leave? Yes, we wanted to start our lives in Greece with the holidays. Christmas is important in Russia, but nothing like what it is in a Christian country like Greece."

He had a rehearsed feel, with smooth answers he thought would settle things. I enjoyed teasing information out, but my pocketful of DNA would establish if he was Boyle's killer. It was time to go, plus, my pee-pee alarm had rung again.

Chapter 34

We sat at our desks reading emails and following leads we knew were worthless. The clock had only moved twenty minutes since my last time check. I needed to know if the DNA on the Wheeler cans or on what I took from Papadakis's were a match. It was impossible to concentrate.

Derrick hung up the phone.

"Geez, this is the second time this woman called in. Now she says she had another dream and that the killer is the mayor of Miami."

"No shortage of people looking for attention. You're single, maybe you can give her what she needs."

"No thanks."

"When did the lab say they'd have the profiles done?"

"This afternoon sometime."

It was only 10:45 a.m. To me, the ticktock of the clock was audible. I had to kill time. My pee alarm went off. It was the first time I was thankful to hear it. I got up to go to the bathroom, knowing it would eat up fifteen minutes.

Sitting on the throne, coaxing my urine out, the status of the Boyle case consumed my mind. It wasn't like I was hoping for a homicide to occur, but with nothing else to distract me I had no choice.

Everything was hinging on the DNA report. Wheeler and Papadakis were the only two suspects we had left. Maybe Detective Foster wasn't as bad an investigator as I thought. Even so, there was no excuse for the way the crime scene and evidence were handled.

Much as I hated to consider the possibility, I had to think about the next steps if the DNA didn't match either of our last candidates. What did we know? A seventeen-year-old girl, getting ready for college, is stabbed to death at a county park. She was with her considerably older boyfriend and her young brother.

Everyone at the park, that we knew about, had been interviewed. All but two were cleared at this point. It had to be one of them. Papadakis was shady. He was guilty of something, but I was leaning toward Wheeler. He was there, and his story smelled like week-old garbage. The MRI proved nothing. He had a head injury, so what? There was no proof it came from a blow the night Boyle was murdered.

I washed up and sent a text to Mary Ann. I had to get out of the office and was hoping she could slip away for an early lunch.

* * *

My office was empty when I returned at twelve thirty. I tapped my mouse and the monitor came alive. There was an email from forensics. The preview pane read: Boyle Case DNA Profiling 2 Complete.

I hesitated before clicking open the email. My finger hovered over the mouse like a poker player squeezing out a card. I dropped my finger and my spirits followed. There was no match to either Wheeler or Papadakis.

I threw my head into the back of my chair. How the hell could that be?

Derrick came in with a box of biscotti. "You want one?"

"No!"

"What's the matter?"

I picked up the phone. "The frigging DNA report came back as no match."

"What? I would've bet it was Papadakis."

"Yeah. Hi, this is Frank Luca. I want to talk with Dempsey . . . When is he going to be back? . . . Well, you tell him to call me as soon as he gets back. It's urgent."

I slammed the phone down. "You have Dempsey's cell number?"

"No. I don't even know him."

"I bet the damn lab screwed up."

"They're pretty good, from what I know."

"Everybody makes mistakes."

"Let's say they didn't and everyone we targeted is not guilty. What do we do next?"

I wanted to say we give up; that's what we do. We put the damn Boyle file away and pluck another cold case out of the box. I really wanted to, but I'd promised the kid's mother I'd get answers for her, and I would.

"What we do is start from scratch. Go over everything, see if we missed something. Keep talking to the mother and the kid's friends. This teenager was murdered at a park; someone has to pay for this. Her mother deserves justice."

"I felt like we were so close."

"Don't give up; we'll get this bastard."

"I know we will. What do you want me to do? Should I stop checking overseas into Papadakis?"

I didn't want to tell him the flossing tool and hair from his bathroom could have been someone else's. "No, keep that line open. He's done something."

"Okay. What else?"

"There was a weird message written in her yearbook by a kid named Fred. I went through and identified three kids that we should talk to. Here, let me show you."

I had a yellow sticky on the message and on each of the pages where a class had a Fred.

Derrick said, "It's not a full-out threat, but it feels like one."

"That's why we have to check it out."

"It could be she dumped him or never returned his affection."

He didn't think I thought of that? "I know that. If it wasn't for the puppy-love angle, we'd have tracked Fred down already."

I handed him the yearbook. "Find Fred and interview him. I have to be somewhere."

* * *

The doctor's office was near Old 41. My appointment was not for another forty minutes. I blew past the turn and headed to Estero.

Making a right off Corkscrew, I slowed down. The garage at the Papadakis house was closed. His dog got up but didn't bark as I drove past. I pulled over about a quarter mile away and waited five minutes before making a U-turn and driving by again. There was no sign of Papadakis, and I left.

Signing in, I chatted with a cute nurse before taking a seat. There was an annoying judge show on the TV. Half the people waiting were riveted to the lowest denominator in the country. The minutia being arbitrated must make them feel superior to the lowlifes on the program.

It was five minutes past my appointed time. I'd been coming to him for over two years, and my appointment time meant as much as one half of a fifty-dollar bill. I couldn't play with my phone any longer and went to the receptionist.

"Hi, I'm sure the doc is busy, but I'm due in court in an hour. Is there anything you can do?"

She smiled. "Let me see, Frank."

Before the court show had a commercial break, my name was called, and I was escorted to an exam room. She weighed me, took my vitals, and I sat on the exam bed, on top of that ridiculous white paper. It didn't even cover the entire surface. With all the technology we have, why we were still relying on preventive measures from the 1940s?

Dr. Brown was a regular guy and a good doctor. Best of all, he was about my age and not an alarmist.

"Hey, Doc. How's it going?"

"Good, Frank. How are you?"

"Pretty good."

"Anything bothering you?"

Could he help with the Boyle case? "No, tired every now and then, but I feel pretty damn good for forty-three."

"You should. They sent me the scan you had, and it's clean."

I exhaled. My oncologist told me it was clear, but after the original diagnosis that I had a small tumor that changed into something much more serious, I craved confirmation.

"That's great."

"You still having a little pinching from the scar tissue?"

"Yeah, but it's not too bad. I kind of got used to it."

"Let me take a look."

He pressed on my stomach and kneaded the area around the scar with his knuckles. "Feels good. You staying on a regular schedule of relieving yourself?"

I tapped my watch. "Have an alarm set to let me know."

"You following it?"

"Most of the time."

He shook his head. "I can't stress the importance of it, Frank. You don't have a bladder, and what they created for you doesn't have the same elasticity. Don't push it, okay?"

"I get it. I'll do better."

"I'd hate to have you ruin all that fancy plumbing they did in there."

"I never asked this, but with all the cutting and pasting I've had done, would any of it prevent me from, say, having a baby?"

Brown eyed me. "No, your reproductive system should not have been affected by the surgery."

I nodded. "Just asking."

"If you're thinking of it, though, the sooner the better. You don't want to be standing on a soccer field when you're sixty. If you want to do something like having kids, you'd better get moving."

My pee-pee alarm rang. I smiled at Dr. Brown, and like a good boy, said, "Time to go to the bathroom." I said goodbye and headed to the bathroom.

Above the toilet was a shelf with scores of urine sample bottles. I sat on the bowl and began thinking.

Sixty? It was only seventeen years away. Seventeen years back I was twenty-six. That seemed like a lifetime ago. I was up in New Jersey and had just graduated from the academy. Time seemed to have sped up. The thought that I'd be sixty was frightening.

What did I want my life to look like at sixty? I wanted to continue as a homicide detective, and the thought of living anywhere else was a nonstarter. Where would Mary Ann and I be? Would one of us get struck with a serious illness? Would my cancer come back?

The day was rare when the thought that my cancer would come back didn't bang around in my head. They said they removed all the cancer, but they had to miss a couple of cells. Didn't they? For a year after my surgery, I'd pictured one cell left behind, furiously dividing, building and growing. I'd lost a lot of sleep over it.

It was Mary Ann who made me realize how destructive those thoughts were. I can still hear her say, "Even though you've had cancer and I haven't, your odds are better than mine. You're being monitored. As soon as something pops up, they'll catch it early. If something is growing in me, I won't know until it starts causing trouble. So, stop worrying about it and live."

She was right, but it was another thing that was easier said than done. I'd avoided thinking about how much she seemed to want kids. She was good about it, or maybe smart was the right word, not trying to push the subject with me. I felt a smile break out when I thought of Billy, the kid next door.

I'd have to think through this having a kid thing. I couldn't sort my thoughts out with the Boyle case taking most of whatever brainpower chemo had left me with. As soon as I was finished with the Boyle case, I'd give the idea serious consideration. Right now, I had to figure out my next move.

Chapter 35

Should I visit Debbie's teachers and ask them about her last day, or that friend of hers who signed the yearbook with that message about Debbie getting through something? I could revisit her girlfriends, pressing them about whatever Debbie might have been going through. It could have been a disagreement with a friend or about losing a friend who was off to an out-of-state college.

They were the only leads, if you could call them leads, I had to pursue. It wasn't quite like trying to smash a pinata while blindfolded, but close enough. I didn't know what direction to go in and resorted to what had worked in the past: revisiting the victim's friends and family.

Many times, with space in between interviews, minds would percolate and generate new information or stories that would provide clues.

One of Debbie Boyle's friends, Nancy Flowers, had been so ill that I never had a chance to interview her. Every time I called, her sister had said she was either in the hospital or too weak to talk. The woman had heart problems and was on the waiting list for a transplant. Talk about serious. It made my bladder cancer feel like a hangnail.

Flowers had been a professor of oceanography at Gulf Coast University and lived in Miromar Lakes, a large, multi-price-point community near the airport. I exited the interstate at Corkscrew Road, and instead of turning right toward Miromar, I decided to ride past the Papadakis house again.

The last two times I drove by, Papadakis was nowhere in sight and the garage was closed. As I crawled down the street, I noticed the garage was open and a man, I assumed was Papadakis, had his back to the street.

As soon as I got out of the car the dog began barking and Papadakis turned around. I waved, and he turned back around, disappearing out of view. I jogged to the garage, and the dog lunged at me. I cut to the left, out of the mutt's reach, as Papadakis shouted, "Down Gorky! Down!"

Growling, the dog sat on its hind legs.

"You really have him under control, don't you?"

"I took him to training classes when he was just a puppy. He's a good boy. Right, Gorky?"

I wasn't about to test that proclamation and inched toward Papadakis, who picked up a nearly empty water bottle.

"What can I do for you, Detective?"

I stepped into the garage. "Was in the neighborhood and figured I'd see if you had a change of heart on the DNA test."

"I haven't. I'm kind of busy at the moment."

The chest was covered by an old shower curtain. "What are you doing?"

"Just cleaning up."

"What do you have in the chest?"

"Family memorabilia."

I lifted the curtain up. "Coming from Russia and Greece, there must be some interesting things in there."

Papadakis set the water bottle down. "Detective, I'd really rather you go. You have no right to be here."

He was right. "I didn't mean to upset you. I was just curious. I've never been out of the country. We're going to Europe in the spring, and maybe it's naïve, but seeing things from a place like Russia seems interesting, that's all."

"Russia back then was anything but interesting. It was depressing."

I backed up to where the water bottle was and said, "Where'd you get Gorky, in Russia?"

Papadakis glanced at his dog, and I pocketed the water bottle, saying "Good boy" to cover the crinkling sound the plastic made.

"Gorky is only four. I got him from a breeder in Venice."

"Nice town, Venice. They kept the old Florida feel up there. Anyway, I'll get moving. See you around."

Papadakis had the puzzled look of someone who'd seen a levitation.

* * *

I flashed my badge to the Miromar guard and circled to Flower's coach home on Valiant Court. Her unit was one of four in a two-story building painted off-white. When the door to the first-floor apartment opened, a makeup-less woman in need of sleep said, "Can I help you?"

My badge ramped up her concern. "Nancy Flowers?"

"No, I'm her sister, Susan. Nancy passed away four days ago."

"Oh, I'm sorry. I didn't know."

"It's okay. I know you were trying to talk to her, but time ran out."

"She couldn't get the transplant?"

"No. It's a crazy system, but Nancy had so many other problems, I don't know if it'd have mattered."

"I'm sorry."

"I know you wanted to talk to her about Debbie Boyle. Maybe I could help. Nancy told everything to her big sister." She smiled.

It couldn't hurt to talk for a few minutes, and this poor woman could certainly use the distraction. "Sure."

I didn't think the place was older than ten years, yet it felt older. The home was built in a style that was getting washed away by a coastal contemporary wave. I put a three-hundred-and-twenty-five-thousand-dollar price on the place.

She led me past a kitchen counter that had two piles of sympathy cards, prompting guilt over my real estate thoughts, and on into a living area where a collapsed walker was propped against a wall.

The sliders were open, and we sat down around the lanai's table. The sun was shimmering off a lake.

"The weather has been just amazing. Zero humidity."

It was either an offer of a drink or the weather that invariably opened most of my visits. "We've had an incredible run of weather. What can you tell me about your sister and Debbie Boyle?"

She rambled on about how close they were. I started drifting away, but she said something that caught me by surprise.

"I'm sorry, I missed that last part about the cheerleading."

"I was saying that the two of them were cheerleaders forever.

Nancy was the captain senior year, and she was mad that Debbie quit the team in the middle of the season."

"Did she know why Debbie quit?"

"I don't think she ever really knew. I think Debbie told her she wasn't having fun doing it. But if you ask me, I think it was that she thought it was, what's the right word, immature. Debbie liked older boys, men really, and cheerleading didn't play well with that set."

"You say she liked men. Others have said she did as well. Is there anyone in particular?"

"I don't know for sure. I was two years older, so I was out of the school, but there were a couple of rumors, and that's all they were."

"What sorts of rumors?"

"Something about her and a teacher or two."

"Male?"

"Yes, and she wasn't the only one that I'd heard about. But in all fairness, it could be just rumors. You know how teenagers can be."

Chapter 36

"Boy, Frank, that was a waste of time."

"You're never wasting time if you're learning. Even when you come up with a zero, it may help to either eliminate a suspect or to close a line of inquiry. What happened?"

"I had to wait around for every one of those guys. But they all said they didn't remember writing anything like that."

"We don't know who wrote that message?"

"No."

"You gotta collect handwriting samples from them."

"You think it's worth doing that?"

"Yep. You never know."

"One of these guys is way the hell up in Winter Gardens and another in Cape Coral."

"What can I tell you? We should know who wrote that message and why."

"You're right, Frank. Sorry about that."

"The bottom line is you just never know what anything leads to. Hey, I dropped a bottle off for DNA testing. Let me know when a report comes in."

"A bottle? From who?"

"Our Russian-Greek creep."

"Papadakis?"

"Yeah."

"But I thought you grabbed some of his DNA already."

"I did, but it came from the bathroom, and I couldn't be sure it was actually his."

"But what about Wheeler? The cans I took, we don't know that he drank from them."

"All three cans had the same DNA, and Wheeler is the root beer drinker."

"When you circle back to the three Freds, ask them about rumors that a male teacher may have been involved with a student or two."

"Romantically? Sexually?"

"Unknown, but I'd guess both."

"Debbie Boyle?"

"Could be."

"Where'd you hear this?"

"A sister of one of Boyle's friends."

"Wow. That would be huge."

"If it was true, yes, but sex between teachers and students is nothing new and is a world away from murder."

"I know. But still, it's crazy to think that a teacher would take advantage of a kid."

"I don't have to remind you that there are a lot of sick individuals walking the planet."

"Amen."

"Don't be spreading this around. I don't want it getting back to the mother before I ask her about it."

"No problem."

"Why don't you go home? You have a lot of driving to do tomorrow."

* * *

I could hear Amy Winehouse singing from the garage. Opening the door to the house, I was greeted with the smell of mushrooms sautéing in garlic and oil. My stomach panged. Pasta and mushrooms were quickly climbing my favorite dish ladder.

The first time I had it was at Molto on Fifth Avenue. I couldn't remember the Italian name for the dish, but it had something to do with tempting priests. A wine tip I had read the week before, that mushrooms and Pinot Noir were a perfect pairing, popped into my head.

Mary Ann was in front of a skillet in shorts so short you could see the lower curve of her ass. I didn't know what to go for first, a handful of her butt or a forkful of mushrooms.

"Smells good." I kissed the nape of her neck and pressed into her backside.

"Easy, Frank, or the mushrooms will burn."

I snuck my hand under her shirt. "I don't care. Let 'em burn."

She pushed me back with her butt. "Yeah, right, for the next five minutes. What kind of pasta you want, fusilli, bow tie, or penne?"

"Fusilli. You want me to grill anything for you?"

"There's a Tupperware in the fridge with shrimp marinating."

I put the grill on, changed, and popped a Siduri pinot noir.

Dinner was great, but the wine was finished. I needed something heavier and opened a French Syrah that Bleu Cellars had recommended. I had a glass as we cleaned up. Life couldn't be better. But that wasn't going to stop me from trying. I put the spa on and coerced Mary Ann into changing into a bathing suit.

Wine glasses in hand, we slipped into the bubbling water.

"We should do this more often." I put my arm around her shoulder. "You've got the body of a teenager."

"Young girls turn you on, Detective?"

"Speaking of that. You've been in Naples a long time. Do you recall any rumors about teachers at the high school having relationships with their students?"

"Having sex with them?"

"Yeah."

"I don't think so. Is this about the Boyle case?"

"Yeah, a sister of a friend of Debbie's said there were rumors about it."

"That would have been twenty-five years or more ago. Unlike you, I wasn't even a teenager then."

"You trying to rub it in?"

"Depends on what needs rubbing."

I put my hand between her thighs.

She wriggled free. "Not now, Frank."

"Is that a promise for later?"

"Maybe."

"You're such a tease."

We talked about her new position on the Cyber Crimes Team until the timer on the spa wound down and the bubbles died off. We could hear the kid next door playing with his dog. I said, "Sounds like Billy is giving Buttercup a workout."

"He's so cute. Yesterday, I went to get the mail, and he was walking the dog with Mary. I tagged along with them."

"He's a good kid."

"He is. It's up to the parents; they make the difference."

"You're right."

"You'd make a great father, Frank."

Is she kidding? I'm about as self-centered as you could imagine. "I don't know about that."

"Well, I do. There's no doubt in my mind."

I knew I had to be careful or I'd ruin the night. I said nothing.

"Frank, it's really something we should talk about before it's too late."

Did she and Dr. Brown talk today? "About what?"

"Whether we should consider having a child."

The water suddenly felt cold. "I guess so."

She took my hand. "I'm not talking right away, but if it's something we both want, then we should talk about it."

"I've been thinking about it."

"You have?"

"Just a little. I know you'd like to be a mom, and I've been giving the whole thing some thought. Not a lot, but you know . . ."

"It's something we shouldn't rush into. But we need to watch the clock if we want to be young-enough parents. I don't want to go to open school night and look like a grandmother."

Open school nights? "We have a couple of years before we have to worry about that."

"At the maximum. You're forty-three, Frank. And say we had a baby two years from now, when our kid was ten you'd be fifty-five."

"Thanks, I needed that."

"It's just a fact, but you're as young as you act."

And I was great at acting immature. "I know, but it catches up to you. You can act however you want at eighty, but you're still eighty and not playing football."

"That's true, to a point, but just don't get hung up on it. Give it some thought, okay?"

I nodded.

"Don't worry, Frank, I won't push you into anything."

"Thanks."

"Let's get out of here."

I wanted to really get out of here after that discussion. We toweled off, and I suggested she shower. She bit, and before Mary Ann knew it, I was in with her.

Chapter 37

Sitting behind my desk steadied me. Mary Ann never mentioned the subject of kids the rest of the night, but it was in the air. Even when we were having sex I couldn't stop thinking that I might be doing it soon as a mission, not as a pleasure.

I sipped my coffee and was reading an email from an old buddy up in Jersey when Derrick came in.

"Good morning. You have a good night?" He put a Starbucks cup on my desk.

Was he in on it too? "Thanks."

"I'm gonna blow out of here in half an hour."

"Yeah, let the rush hour traffic on 75 die down."

"You have anything for me?"

"No. Just bring in the handwriting samples, and don't forget to ask about the teacher-student sex thing."

"Got it covered. I can't imagine making it back here before seven."

I popped off the coffee lid. It was perfect. It'd been a while since he'd screwed up. "Go straight home. You can drop it at the lab in the morning."

"Thanks. What are you up to today?"

"I'm thinking about going back to see the mother, or maybe Boyle's girlfriends."

"Oh, I almost forgot. I picked up three more cans of root beer from Wheeler's recycling bin."

I gave him a thumbs-up. "You can never be too careful."

"I thought about what you said, and it made perfect sense."

"It doesn't pay to take chances or get sloppy. You're going to make a fine homicide detective. Why don't we kick around what this kid Fred could've meant when he wrote 'You're going to regret it.'?"

"I think he probably wanted to date her, and she rejected him."

"Or it could've been as simple as the college or major she was going for."

"Could there be a link to that and what her other friend said about she'd always be there for her? Like she was going to do something, and Fred said it was a bad move, and the other girl offered her support?"

It was a stretch, but thinking out of the box was what made a good detective. "Outside chance, but doubtful. Hey, before I forget, it seems that Boyle quit cheerleading in the middle of the season. See if any Fred knows something about why."

* * *

I looked over the offerings at the Second Cup Coffee shop. It was between a bagel and a croissant. With the Paris trip ahead, I opted for the French pastry and a dark roast as I waited for Joanne Wilbur. Debbie Boyle's old friend was showing a client a couple of apartments at Mercato.

Picking at a remaining flake, I saw her come through the doors. She pushed her sunglasses to the top of her head and flashed a smile. We exchanged hellos.

"Would you like a cup of coffee?"

"Definitely. The couple I just left were exhausting. They found an issue with everything. If I found them a palace on the beach for a million, they'd find something wrong with it."

"You find that, call me first. Medium or dark roast?"

I handed her a coffee, and she reached into her bag, pulling out a purplish packet. She emptied the contents into her cup and stirred it. People were going to extremes to control what they put in their bodies.

She took a sip, smearing the cup with lipstick. "Thanks, I needed that. So, how is the investigation going?"

"We're working it hard, and it's why I wanted to talk with you again."

"Anyway I can help, I will. You know, you look like George Clooney, don't you?"

I smiled. That was the third Clooney reference in a month. Maybe sixty wasn't as close as I thought. "I hear that from time to time. You said you were on the cheerleading squad with Debbie."

"Yes, we were."

"I was told that she quit in the middle of the last season. I'm interested in knowing why."

"We were surprised when she quit. She never really gave a reason. One time Debbie told me she was tired of it and that it was immature, but she told others that her ankle was bothering her and didn't want to risk it."

"What did you think?"

"I thought it was strange, but I figured she was moving on, putting some distance between her and high school."

"Who was Fred?"

"Fred? What's the last name?"

"I'm not sure yet, but he was the guy who wrote 'You're going to regret it' in her yearbook."

"I didn't know about that, and I don't like the way it sounds. I think she would have told me, though."

"Did Debbie keep secrets?"

She tilted her head and an earring came into view. "We all have secrets, don't we?"

"Was one of her secrets that she was having a relationship with a teacher?"

Coffee spilled onto the table. "Oh, I'm sorry." She grabbed a handful of napkins and cleaned up the spill.

"Was Debbie Boyle in a relationship with a teacher?"

"We all had crushes on teachers from time to time, but I don't think she did anything like what you're inferring."

"But she liked older men; you said that the last time we chatted."

"Yeah, but I also said that all of us liked older boys. It's not unusual at that age."

She had a sharp recollection that I'm sure she put to good use selling homes.

"Were there rumors at the high school about a teacher or teachers that may have crossed the line with a student or two?"

"Sexually?"

"Yes."

"I don't think so."

"Is there anything else you can tell me?"

"Not really, but did you ever check into Jason Norwicky?"

Damn it. I'd forgotten about that kid. I was so focused on Moore that Norwicky fell victim to my chemo brain.

"I'm sorry, Ms. Wilbur, but I can't talk about an ongoing investigation."

Chapter 38

Racing back to the office, I couldn't shake the blues. How the hell did I forget to check into Norwicky? Boyle pissed him off after she led him on, and then she embarrassed him in the schoolyard. Male teenagers couldn't take that kind of public disrespect. If this were the Chicago inner city, he would have probably shot her right then and there. And the way Chicago was going, he'd probably get away with it.

This wasn't Chicago, thank God, but Collier County. Violence didn't have borders, but would a scorned teen wait months before acting? I slowed down. Chances were, he'd forgotten about it in a couple of weeks.

The blue cloud lifted until I remembered the serial killer I'd caught. Talk about patience, the revenger waited years to even the score. I'd have to look into Norwicky fast or risk a sleepless night. There was still time today to track him down.

*　*　*

The court database had nothing on Jason Norwicky; he had never been arrested. I doubted our new record management system would have anything, and it didn't.

People's desire to drive was the cover governments used to keep track of you. The Department of Motor Vehicles had information that amounted to an identity card. I didn't like the government knowing too much about me, but as a law enforcement officer, I couldn't imagine not having the DMV as a resource.

I typed Jason Norwicky into their portal. Nothing came up. He probably moved out of state. The national database for problem drivers also came up empty. This damn case wouldn't even allow me to take the simplest shortcut.

I ran a quick property search, and there was nothing again. Time to look on social media. Everybody these days was on Facebook, except me and Mary Ann, and now, Norwicky. Was I chasing a ghost? I sent a text to Mary Ann, asking her to check other channels, and I dug deeper.

The last known address the Collier school system had for Norwicky was in a community off Orange Blossom Road called Sunshine Village. It was an old development with a lot of disorienting red brick. Mature trees provided plenty of shade, and most of the grass had given way to moss.

A pair of ten-year-olds were playing catch in front of my target address. Chances were the Norwicky family had moved. After confirming my feelings, I surveyed the block, looking for homes that hadn't been updated.

I walked to the door of a yellow stucco and brick house with a gnome standing guard. I was two for two; the woman who opened the door was in her sixties.

"Good afternoon, ma'am. I'm with the sheriff's department, and I'm looking for the Norwicky family."

"Really? They moved a long time ago."

"Can you give me an idea how long ago?"

"Oh, it was way back. Sometime after that poor girl was found dead."

"Debbie Boyle, at Delnor-Wiggins?"

"Yes. That was her. We were all shocked. My kids went to school with her, as did a few others in here."

"Do you know where they went?"

"I'm not sure, but maybe my daughter would know. I can call her."

"That'd be nice of you. What can you tell me about Jason Norwicky?"

"Jason? He was a nice boy. It was a shame he had what he did."

"What was that?"

"Epilepsy."

That was why he couldn't drive. "How bad was his epilepsy?"

"As a child it was terrible. A couple of times when he was here he had seizures, but over time they fine-tuned the medication and he was much better."

"Do you know where the family moved to?"

"Oh boy, I kinda remember them moving to Bonita, but let me check with my daughter."

She called her daughter, shook her head, and left a message.

"Here's my card. Please call me as soon as you speak with your daughter."

* * *

Derrick had a glum look and a new haircut. "Hey, boss. What's going on?"

"Something new and interesting just surfaced." It wasn't new, but it was interesting. "A Jason Norwicky had an altercation with our victim in school. Seems like she led him on, and when he followed up she rejected him. It turned physical, and this Norwicky kid ended up getting embarrassed in front of the entire school."

"Where did you find that out?"

"A friend of Boyle's—I saw her earlier." That was true.

"He wasn't in the original investigation. I would have remembered a name like that. It sounds promising."

"We'll see. I'm trying to track him down."

"What do you mean?"

"He's a virtual ghost at this point, no record of him, he doesn't even have a license."

"What about a last known?"

"I went to his old neighborhood, back when the homicide occurred. I'm hoping a neighbor's kid has something we can follow."

"Nothing on social media?"

"Zippo on Facebook, but I have Vargas checking around."

"Think this guy disappeared right after killing her?"

"We'll find out."

"Frank, this could be it. Someone who fought with her; he's got motive, and then he disappears. It's got to be him."

"Hold on, Derrick."

"But you told me if my gut tells me, not to ignore it."

"You just learned about this, kid. That's not your gut but a knee-jerk reaction. We can't lose focus every time we run into a person of interest. We've got to be methodical, keep chasing and eliminating. We'll get our guy."

"I, uh, it just sounded like he was the perfect fit."

"What did you get from the Freds?"

"Dropped off samples of their handwriting to the lab for analysis."

"Anybody resist giving it to you?"

"Not really. They all claimed not to have written in her yearbook."

"What about the rumors of teacher and student relationships?"

"Nothing, really. Just some comments that there was apparently a woman teacher who was pretty hot."

"But what about a male teacher?"

"Just that there were two teachers that the girls all liked, a Mr. Stark and a Mr. Culver."

"Culver was the one involved in the SAT test dustup."

"Yeah, that's right, but it's got nothing to do with anything."

"Do me a favor, check with the lab on the Papadakis bottle. I'm due to take a piss."

Chapter 39

After I went to the bathroom, I grabbed a coffee in the cafeteria. Stepping back to the office, I paused. Derrick was talking to a woman with chestnut hair and a boy about seven years old.

"Oh, here's my partner, Detective Frank Luca. Frank, this is my sister Paula and my nephew Bert."

Bert? Who names a kid Bert? "Nice to meet you." I went to shake his sister's hand, but the little boy stepped up, and I took his extended hand.

"You have a strong handshake, Bert."

"Uncle Derrick said you're teaching him how to catch killers. Can you teach me too?"

"Well, you need to be a little bit older."

"But I'm eight and a half already."

"You're almost there, then. They won't let me teach anyone until they're twenty-one."

"That's so far away. I want to be a policeman."

"The rules are the rules, I'm afraid, but you seem to have potential, so let me see what I can do. I'll be right back."

We had a community outreach program that I really liked. It humanized officers on the street and helped build trust in us. I ducked into the office and picked up a couple of items.

My hands were behind my back when I came back in.

"Officer Bert."

The kid turned around, and I handed him a plastic badge. "Here's your badge. You're an official junior deputy for the Collier County Sheriff's Department."

The kid had a grin fit for a jack-o'-lantern. "Mom! Look at my badge. Put in on me, hurry."

"Hold on, Officer, you'll need your hat." I put the hat on, and it fell over his ears. I adjusted the Velcro and fit in on his head.

"Mom, this is so cool. Take a picture, and send it to Daddy."

Derrick mouthed a thank you as a picture was taken.

"Take one of me and the detective, hurry."

The kid sidled up to me and I knelt down.

"Derrick, why don't you take Officer Bert on a tour. Maybe the sheriff can say hello."

"Oh boy, the sheriff? I can meet the real sheriff?"

"If he's not busy solving a crime, I'm sure he'd like to meet his newest junior deputy."

The kid grabbed his uncle's hand and began marching out the door when he turned around and gave me a salute. I returned the salute and stood there for a solid two minutes. The kid was amazing.

I was feeling something. It wasn't pride that I'd made a kid happy; it was jealousy, and it was stupid.

I collapsed into my chair and checked emails. Clicking on one from forensics, my mood took another step lower. The water bottle I took from Papadakis wasn't a match, and neither were the Wheeler root beer cans.

Two of the strongest suspects were in the clear. Or were they? Was the DNA under the victim's fingernail the deciding factor? By all accounts, Boyle was a fighter and would have resisted her attacker. But if she knew the killer and was surprised by him or her, maybe she wouldn't have been able to claw at them.

I thought about Wheeler. His story bothered me. It wasn't his DNA under the nail, and if he did have a slight skull fracture, it may or may not have occurred that night. If not for his story, the physical side of things would have led me to lay off him.

Papadakis had a middle name, and it wasn't Greek or Russian. He'd have you believe it was Unlucky. The reality was that teenagers turned up dead no matter what continent he was on.

Letting the two of them go was something I wasn't prepared to do at this point. I'd give them room as we continued to look under rocks. The phone rang. It was the Norwicky neighbor I had visited.

"That's okay. I'm glad you called . . . Did you speak with your daughter? . . . What? . . . Is she sure? . . . When did this happen? . . . Where? . . . I know you didn't. Please give me your number and your daughter's, in case I need to speak with either of you."

Chapter 40

"Man, you should have seen Chester with Bert. I didn't think the sheriff had much of a personality, but damn, he acted like he worked for Disney—"

"Norwicky is dead."

"What?"

"Jason Norwicky, the kid who fought with Boyle and disappeared, is dead."

"When? How?"

"He died from a massive heart attack about eleven years ago."

"I can't believe it. He could be our guy. Now what?"

I wanted to tell him how I really felt, like someone trying to tie a bow tie in the dark with one hand.

"We're going to dig in, see what else we can learn about him. Find out the circumstances that led to him moving. See if there was anything else between him and Boyle."

"But if he's the killer, he'll never be brought to justice."

"I'm sure Mrs. Boyle would like to be a witness to the death penalty for the killer, but if it was Norwicky, maybe God got the ultimate revenge. I just hope it's good enough for that poor woman."

"My first homicide, and we're chasing a dead man?"

"We don't know that, but we could be. Say, I'm sorry for cutting you off about your nephew. That kid was something else."

"Thanks for being so nice to him. You made his day. I didn't know we had stuff for kids here."

"Your sister's lucky to have him, and you as an uncle. It must be fun to take him around and teach him things."

"Last spring I brought him up to Fort Myers to see the Red Sox. It was his first game. I bought him a baseball, and he collected more autographs in one day than I did in ten years."

"Even the players can't resist a cute kid."

"You think you'll ever have kids, Frank?"

I shrugged. "Who knows?"

"You're supposed to know."

"Seeing a kid like your nephew makes me say yes, but I don't know. It'd be a whole new way of life."

"How about Mary Ann?"

"She's a definite yes. But she's good, you know; she doesn't push it too hard."

"I'm no expert, but I think you'd better make sure you're on the same page. Something like this can screw things up between you both in the future."

He was right. If I prevented her from having a kid, I'd pay for it in boatloads of resentment, eventually ruining our relationship.

* * *

The forensic document examiner placed a magnifying sheet over the specimen. "You see here, Frank, the curve in this loop doesn't quite match. But my opinion is that the difference was intentional."

"Intentional? You mean trying to make his handwriting different than usual?"

"Precisely. Look here, the upward swing is natural, but over here it's forced; a slower pace was used in the stroke."

I don't know how the hell he could infer that. One looked like it had a tiny vibrato to it, but that was all. "You're sure about that?"

"I'm certain, though with two caveats. I understand the original is twenty-five years old. Many factors could naturally alter a person's handwriting, like a nervous or muscle disease or an affliction of the eye."

Certain and caveat in the same sentence? Was he a politician? "You mentioned two exceptions."

"The other is the psychological condition of the writer. I'm no graphologist, but your handwriting can be affected by your state of mind."

Great. I needed a handwriting shrink. "I don't know if I want to go there. If I took it into court, it would get shredded."

"True."

"Okay, the bottom line is you believe this sample was written by the same person who left the note in the yearbook?"

"Exactly. Though there are differences between the two, the person who tended this sample purposely wrote it in a way to mask his natural style."

* * *

As soon as I got back to my office I popped Freddy Palmer into the system. There weren't any police records, not even for a touch like a car accident. Property records provided two hits. I cross-referenced them in DMV: one Freddy Palmer was only thirty-two; the other was forty, with glasses, and was our man.

Mary Ann had let me know that Derrick mentioned his desire to go on more interviews with me. He was right, and I wanted him to get more experience. Problem was, he wasn't due back from the shooting range for another hour.

Freddy Palmer lived off Livingston Road in an area now tagged Livingston Estates. His expansive property was named Nautical Ranch. I rang the call box at the gate and it swung open. The gravel drive meandered past a barn and a large pen with three horses. A pickup was hooked up to a horse trailer, blocking the entrance to the large home.

A pair of ten-foot, mahogany doors were framed by a pair of cypress trees. The wind blew a billow of dust across the driveway. As I surveyed the property, the door swung open. A man with a shaved head, glasses, and a smile said, "You're with the police?"

I showed him my badge. "Yes, Detective Luca, and you are?"

"Freddy Palmer. What's going on?"

"I'd like to ask you a couple of questions."

Palmer leaned back. "About what?"

"Debbie Boyle."

"I already told that other detective I didn't know anything about it."

The sun was beating on my back. "I know, but the case has been reopened, and we're essentially starting from scratch."

Palmer blinked twice and shook his head. "But that was over twenty years ago."

"May I come in?"

He stepped to the side. "Let's go to my office."

The house had a terracotta tile floor and a Mediterranean feel. A pair of large paintings of Spanish galleons dominated the foyer.

Palmer's office was a modern affair. A huge glass desk with four monitors blinking numbers and symbols in green and red. This guy was a trader of some sort.

"What do you do for a living?"

"Currency trader."

"I hear you got to get up pretty early to trade the European markets."

He smiled. "True, but I get to quit early and ride my horses. Now, how can I help you?"

I took a sheet of paper out and put it on his desk. "You wrote this in Debbie Boyle's yearbook. Why?"

He shook his head. "Like I told the other detective, I never wrote that. I hardly even knew her. There were five hundred kids in the school."

"She was a popular kid, a cheerleader. You're telling me you didn't know her?"

"I knew who she was, but that was about it. As far as cheerleading goes, I didn't play sports then or now. What is it you think I did?"

"Read the message. It's a threat."

He slid the paper toward me. "It could mean anything, but I wouldn't know because I didn't write it."

"Handwriting experts disagree."

"You went to a handwriting expert? What the hell is going on here?"

My pee-pee alarm sounded, and I snoozed it. "Just trying to understand what you meant by it."

He threw his hands up. "How many times do I have to tell you, I didn't write that message."

"Where were you the night Debbie Boyle was murdered?"

He tucked his chin in and hesitated. "I—I think I went to the movies. Yeah, that was it."

"What did you see?"

There was that blinking again. "*Jurassic Park*."

He had the right movie for 1993, but that didn't mean he saw it that night.

"Who did you go with?"

"Are you kidding me? You're treating me like a damn suspect."

"Who did you go to the movies with?"

"Steve Bueller."

As I jotted down the name, he said, "You know, if you're looking for a damn Fred, why don't you look into Mr. Stark. His first name is Fred."

"Are you talking about Fred Stark, the teacher?"

"Yes."

Chapter 41

An hour past my deadline, I sat on the throne and tickled my swollen belly. Hoping relief would come fast, I pondered the Boyle case. We had two newbies to look into, Norwicky and Stark, but I was uneasy. I couldn't put my finger on it. Was I dealing with some sleazebag who took advantage of girls? Was it my cop instincts or my paternal instincts flaring up?

Urine started to trickle as I wondered if I should follow up on Norwicky first. If it turned out a dead man did it, I'd avoid getting involved with the school and the teacher's union, not to mention possibly making accusations that were unfounded. Plus, if it leaked out, and it always leaked out, I'd put a stain on some guy's reputation that would follow him to the cemetery.

But if there was something going on, I couldn't let the pervert continue. The last drops of pee dripped out as I settled on a middle ground.

"Derrick, I want you to start on Norwicky. Go see his parents, find out why they moved, why their son left. See if they remember where he was the night of the murder. If they give you something on an alibi, I wanted it vetted so there's absolutely no doubt. Can you do that?"

"Of course, I can. Don't you trust me?"

"You're my partner; that's bigger than trust."

"Thanks."

"What I really want is DNA from the parents. We'd know if it was their son's DNA under her nail. But I don't want to push it. Let's see what you come up with before we ramp it up."

"I've got it."

* * *

Riding north on Airport Road, I made a left onto Cougar Drive, the access road for Barron Collier High School. Named for the patriarch of the family for whom the county was named, the school looked the forty-plus years it was.

It was well maintained, but the styling and cinder block construction spoke of another generation, one that Debbie Boyle had been a part of.

I walked down the center of an upside-down U toward the blue tiled entrance. It was eerily quiet for a building housing hundreds of teenagers. The doors were locked, and I hit the bell.

The hallway floor reflected fluorescent lights as I passed classroom after classroom. I could hear muffled voices as I passed their doorways. One door was open, and the teacher, who was reciting a poem, looked my way as I passed. A few paces away I reached my destination.

I stared at the sign on the administrative office. It read: Principal Larry Culver. The teacher had gotten a major upgrade in twenty-five years. I pushed the door open, announcing myself. As the receptionist summoned Stark, I scanned the office looking for Culver. He didn't appear to be in, and I was shown into a conference room.

I sat in the windowless room waiting for Mr. Stark. He was under the impression we were meeting about one of his students. The element of surprise was a cliché, but I enjoyed using it.

Fred Stark may have been cute in 1993, but I had a hard time believing that this balding man could have attracted Debbie Boyle. He was built like an ostrich: skinny legs, potbelly, and long neck.

We shook hands, and he sat across the Formica table.

"I'm hoping one of my students hasn't gotten into too deep a mess. But your presence belies that, doesn't it?"

"My visit relates to an old student of yours."

His face relaxed. "Oh, that's good. Who is it then?"

"Debbie Boyle."

Was that fear or sadness that flashed across his face?

"Oh, I'd heard the case was reopened. How can I help?"

"How well did you know Debbie Boyle?"

He stroked his chin. "She was in my class, I think it was her junior year. Yeah, it had to be because it wasn't her last, uh, senior year. She was a good student. I think she was a cheerleader as well."

"Was she friendly?"

"Friendly? Yeah, I believe so. She was a pretty popular girl."

"Pretty or popular?"

"I don't understand."

"Did you think she was pretty? A good-looking girl?"

"I guess so."

"Were you attracted to her?"

Starks eyes narrowed. "Excuse me?"

"It's my understanding that, back in the day, a lot of the schoolgirls thought you were cute."

Stark patted his belly. "They should see me now."

He was right about that. "Did you ever try to explore Debbie Boyle's interest in you?"

"Now, hold on a minute, Detective. I don't like the direction this is going. Are you trying to imply that I had an inappropriate relationship with a student?"

"It's something we've received information on."

"About me? What information?"

"We've been told that there may have been a couple of male teachers who crossed the line with female students."

"And you think I was one of them?"

So, it wasn't rumor. "Did you have a relationship with Debbie Boyle?"

"None other than what a concerned teacher has with a student."

Concerned? Why the modifier? "Did she come to you with her personal problems?"

"I encourage all my students, male and female, to talk to me about their lives. I want them to feel comfortable confiding in me."

"What did Debbie Boyle share with you?"

"Nothing memorable. She was concerned, like all kids, about what her future would look like. She was torn between choosing a life like her mother's and shooting higher. I think she wanted to take a run at life but was afraid to leave her widowed mother behind."

He knew a lot about her. "And what advice did you give her?"

"The same I give all my students: follow your heart and dreams. I encourage them to live in a way that allows them the opportunity to reach their fullest potential."

I pulled out the yearbook picture. "What did you mean when you wrote this?"

He eyed the message and then me. He looked at the paper again and set it down. "I don't know what's going on here, but it's making me uncomfortable. I didn't write this."

"Are you sure?"

"Of course I am. It's not my handwriting, and school policy refrains teachers from signing students' yearbooks."

That was a lie. There were several other messages from teachers in Boyle's book.

Before I could respond there was a knock on the door before it swung open. A sandy-haired man, with squared shoulders and jaw, stepped into the room. His hazel eyes sparkled when he said, "Is everything okay here?"

Stark said, "Detective Luca, this is the school principal, Larry Culver."

I stood and shook his hand. "Good to meet you, Mr. Culver."

"Likewise. I understand a student of Mr. Stark's has gotten into trouble. Is there anything the school needs to be concerned about, besides the student's welfare?"

"Not at the moment, Mr. Culver. We're finished here, but can I have a minute of your time?"

Culver looked at his watch. "I have twenty minutes before a staff meeting."

"That's more than I need."

"Fred, why don't you head back to class while I speak with the detective."

I followed Culver into a generous office with a bank of windows overlooking a ball field. Besides a glossy ceramic apple and a nameplate, his desk was empty.

"Make yourself comfortable. You want a coffee or something?"

"No thanks."

Culver settled into his chair as I scanned the credenza behind it. Four photos of a girl. He had a daughter.

"What brings you to Barron Collier High?"

"It's come to our attention that in the early nineties there were inappropriate relationships between teachers and students."

Culver studied me for a moment. "Inappropriate?"

"Of a sexual nature."

"Oh, come now, Detective, you're telling me that a teacher here"—he tapped his desk with a forefinger—"had sex with a student?"

"Exactly, and it's teachers, not teacher."

He frowned.

"You were a teacher back then, don't tell me there were no rumors about it."

"Rumors were all they were."

"Are you sure?"

He shrugged. "There was a teacher back then that a lot of the girls liked, and there was no doubt he liked the attention, but that's all I know."

"What's his name?"

"Morgan. Peter Morgan, but he's long gone."

"Was one of the girls who liked him Debbie Boyle?"

He hesitated. "You know what? Now that I think of it, she was."

"I'd like to take a look at his record and get his last known address."

"Sure, come on."

As we left his office I stopped and stared at the college diploma on the wall. It was from Rutgers University.

Chapter 42

I couldn't stop thinking about the Rutgers link. Debbie Boyle had a ring from Rutgers, and now we had a teacher who graduated from Rutgers. Was it a coincidence or a connection? It needed exploring, but first I wanted to follow up on Peter Morgan.

Morgan was living in Jacksonville and teaching at Robert E. Lee High School. He'd only taught at Barron Collier High for two years. As I inputted what I knew about Morgan into the murder book, I kept wondering what made him leave so quickly.

As I considered my next move, Derrick came into the office waving a crayon drawing.

"Bert made this for you."

It was a blue police car with a red ball on its roof and two stick figures beside it. In the speech balloon above the car, Bert had written, "Me and Detective Frank."

"You have a new buddy."

"I'm going to have to get this framed. I could use some pictures around here."

"I know, it's like you don't have a life outside this place."

"I like to keep things separate, you know?" I hoped he wouldn't crush that theory by asking why I was living with my ex-partner.

He raised an eyebrow and sat behind his desk.

"What did you get on Norwicky?"

"Parents sold the house in 2001, almost eight years after the Boyle murder. Their son Jason left to go to Florida State University in Tallahassee after graduating. They said he left in late July."

"What was your sense of them?"

"I believed them."

"Belief comes with facts, not feelings. Call FSU and see when

Norwicky got there. Now, what about an alibi for him on the night of the murder?"

"They said they couldn't remember."

"See?"

"See what? They're in their seventies."

"Things like a murder burn into your memory. You'd remember what you were doing if someone you knew, someone your kid was friends with, was murdered. This isn't New York, where a body shows up like the sun each day. Especially back in 1993, this town was a lot smaller."

"You're just like President Reagan: trust but verify."

"Exactly. You should know that. How much bullshit did you hear up in DC?"

"Endless. You're right. You want me to get some DNA samples?"

"No other way to be positive it isn't him."

"Should I just ask them outright, or grab what I can?"

"That's your call. I don't care how you get it, as long as you do."

"Got it."

"On second thought, don't ask them. See what opportunities there are to get a sample from them."

"Why the change of heart?"

"They've been through enough losing a son. If their kid wasn't involved, I don't want to stress them out."

"You're right."

"Hey, do me a favor, check out Rutgers University up in Jersey. See how many graduates they churn out and how big their teaching degree department is."

"I'm on it."

As he tapped away, I completed a page on Morgan.

"Wow. Rutgers has been around forever. It was started back in 1766, before we were even a country."

How was that going to help the investigation? "I didn't know that."

"It's huge. Fifty thousand students, plus another twenty in their grad programs."

"How big was it back in 1984?"

"Tough to say exactly, but looks like in the low thirty thousand range, plus the graduate program. Bigger than most towns."

"How many teacher degrees did they give out in 1984?"

"I'm going to have to call for that. But even if it was just ten percent, that'd be a couple of thousand."

"Forget it. Don't waste any more time on it. Get back to Norwicky."

* * *

Jacksonville was a good seven hours away with moderate traffic. About to tell Derrick to take the ride, I saw the picture his nephew had made for me and broke my own protocol by using the phone.

When I heard Peter Morgan's smoker voice, I was glad to have dodged the second-hand smoke. I introduced myself and followed with, "I'd like to ask you a couple of questions about your time at Barron Collier High."

"That was ages ago."

"Did you know a student by the name of Debbie Boyle?"

"Sure, the poor kid was murdered right after I left."

"After you left the school?"

"Yes. I left about a month before she was killed."

"And why did you leave the area?"

"My mother had early onset Alzheimer's, and I moved to Jacksonville to help my dad out."

"And you're certain that was before the Boyle homicide."

"Absolutely."

"Where did you go to college?"

"FSU."

I heard a match striking. "I understand you were the object of a lot of attention from the female students when you were there."

"What do you mean?"

"That a lot of girls had a crush on you."

"Me? Who told you that?"

"Larry Culver."

"Culver? That's crazy. I hear he's the principal now."

"He is."

"You should ask him. Between Fred Stark and him, they had half the girls in the school eating out of their hands."

"Do you believe either one of them had an inappropriate relationship with any of the students?"

"I don't know for sure, but it's certainly possible. The flirting used to piss me off."

"Do you think either of them could have had something going on with Debbie Boyle?"

"I don't know about Stark, but I saw Culver and her together several times."

"Alone?"

"Just once in his classroom, but other times with another girl or two."

"When they were alone that time, what did you observe?"

"They weren't doing anything. He was sitting behind his desk, and she was to the side. But they were uncomfortable; there was tension. The kid wouldn't look at me. I got the sense she'd been crying."

Chapter 43

Mary Ann was sitting in my recliner when I dropped the picture in her lap.

"What's this?"

"Derrick's nephew Bert made it for me."

"When did you meet him?"

"A couple of days ago. He came into the office with his mother. The kid was something else. I picked up a badge and hat from the neighborhood outreach for him, and he went nuts."

"That was nice of him to make this for you. You made an impression on him."

"Bert said he wants to be a police officer."

"You didn't discourage him, did you?"

"I would never do that. Kids should decide for themselves."

"You'd make a good father, Frank."

"I don't know about that."

"Well, I do. A child would be lucky to have you play with them and guide them through life. Having a dad like you is so important to a kid's development. I know it's no guarantee, but it goes a long way toward making sure a child grows into a healthy adult."

"I'm not changing the subject"—even though I was—"but the Boyle girl, she lost her father as a young kid. She gravitated toward older boys, but what about a teacher?"

"Very possible. A teacher is the head of the class, a leader who teaches kids and looks out for their welfare."

"It's the last part I'm struggling with. If the relationship crossed a line, became sexual . . ."

"You think she may have been involved with a teacher?"

"Something was going on at that school. But whether it involved

Boyle or had anything to do with her death is what I'm going to find out."

* * *

Back in Pelican Landing, I parked in front of Janet Lipton's home. The color of the house reminded me of Boar's Head mustard. A landscaper was cutting the lawn and shut the mower off as I approached. Ringing the bell, I studied the tubular wind chime. There were little Kokopelli figures etched into each tube. With the chime swaying, they looked like they were dancing.

"You like our chime?"

"I always got a kick out of flute-playing Kokopelli."

"Well, it worked for us."

"Music?"

"No, Native Americans considered Kokopelli the god of fertility. When we were having trouble having a child, my sister picked this up for us, and I was pregnant a couple of weeks later."

Fertility? Pregnancy? "I didn't know that, but it's a subject I wanted to talk to you about."

She eyed me suspiciously. "Shall we sit out back like the last time?"

"Sure. It's a gorgeous day."

"Go ahead, I'm going to grab us a couple of iced teas."

She was about my age but looked older. Was it the stress from being a parent?

Lipton set down two glasses loaded with ice. I didn't like it when there was too much ice.

"Thanks."

"How is the inquiry going?"

"Good. We're making progress."

"How can I help?"

"Debbie quit the cheerleading team in midseason. Do you know why?"

"She never really said why. We were surprised, but one minute she said her knee was starting to bother her, then she said it was childish to cheer."

"Was anything going on in her life at the time she quit?"

"Nothing comes to mind."

"I'm curious about something. Do you think Debbie might have been in a relationship with a teacher at Barron High?"

She stroked her glass with a finger, making lines in the condensation. "The answer is, I don't know."

"But you think it was possible."

"I guess so."

"Last time we met, you had said you thought she may have been doing something with Father Harrigan, I think it was."

She nodded. "Yes. Debbie liked older men. Authority figures."

"Was it a teacher named Peter Morgan?"

"Peter Morgan? No way. We used to make fun of his yellow teeth and nicotine-stained fingers. He smelled like an ashtray."

I always wondered how someone could be married to a smoker if they didn't smoke.

"How about Fred Stark or Peter Culver?"

Her eyebrows arched. "Mr. Stark and Mr. C were the school heartthrobs, no doubt. And Debbie, well, she was Debbie. She flirted with them all the time."

"You think she could have been, uh, fooling around with both of them?"

"No way."

"But you said she flirted with both of them. Could she have been playing one off the other?"

Her face broke into a smile. "That would be Debbie."

"Did she have a favorite between the two of them?"

"I don't know, though, most girls liked Mr. C. But then again, Debbie wasn't like most of us."

"Was Debbie using any kind of birth control?"

"I don't know."

"Do you think it is possible that Debbie was pregnant at the time of her murder?"

She ran her finger around the rim of the glass. "It's possible; she was sexually active."

Chapter 44

We were carrying in bags of groceries that Mary Ann bought at Publix when she yelled, "Ow! I think I broke my funny bone."

"Tell me a joke. I'll see if it's broken."

"I'm not kidding. I banged it right here."

"I'll kiss your boo-boo; it'll make it feel better."

She smiled. "That's what my mother used to tell me when I got hurt. Did I tell you that?"

"No." I took a bottle of Neurofuse out of a bag. "What's this?"

"A supplement. You said the Brainol wasn't working, so I thought you should try something different."

Is that the real reason, or was she noticing my memory was getting worse? "Thanks. You know, I can't stop thinking of Boyle's mother. She had this sadness to her. It's like you're afraid to get too close and catch it, you know?"

"It's not surprising. It doesn't get worse than losing a child. It's incredibly difficult to bounce back from that. I read somewhere that more than half of couples who have a child that dies before thirty end up getting divorced."

"Hmm. That's scary."

"You can't be intimidated by it. The chances are small, but even if not, it's worth it. My mom always said, 'You haven't lived until you've had a child.'"

I didn't know what to say and blurted, "Having a cop as a father isn't easy for a kid, you know."

"It may be easier if both are. Look at Ron and Joan, they have three, and Bill and Lucy; they're both like Disney families."

"That's because you don't really know them."

"What are you talking about?"

"Just that in every house, I don't care how it looks from the outside, every picture is not hanging straight."

"True. I remember there was this family who lived across the street, and they had a daughter a couple of years older than me and a son who was the quarterback for the high school. The father was a doctor and the mother, Miss Volunteer. Then it came out that the girl, who was only fifteen, had gotten pregnant, and the mother was an alcoholic."

"What kinds of things would happen to a girl when she gets pregnant? I know about the nausea, but what other signs would there be?"

"You talking about the Boyle girl?"

I stuffed broccoli rabe in the produce drawer. "Yeah."

"She would have had some vaginal discharge. It would stain her panties."

"Could her mother have mistook it for something from her menstrual cycle?"

"I've never been pregnant, Frank. I really don't know."

"Can you ask a girlfriend?"

"You really think she was pregnant, don't you?"

I couldn't tell her that the Kokopelli gave me a private flute concert. "I'm finding it more likely. It would answer a couple of questions."

"Such as?"

"Why she quit cheerleading, and a possible motive if the person who impregnated her didn't want the baby and she did."

"You think she would have kept the baby? I don't know about that."

"Why do you say that?"

"She just turned seventeen. Her entire life was ahead of her. She was going to college. How was she going to do that with a baby?"

It was a good point. "Maybe she had a change of heart when she found out she was pregnant. She quit cheerleading to protect the baby, didn't she?"

"It was a different time, Frank."

"Exactly! Twenty-five years ago I could see having a baby would change a girl's viewpoint. Today, I don't think they'd hesitate to have an abortion if it got in the way of their plans."

"Damn you, Frank! You're a Neanderthal."

"Don't get so excited, Mary Ann. I'm not passing judgment on anybody."

"The hell you ain't."

"No, I mean it. I'm just trying to figure this homicide out, that's all."

"A woman has a right do what she wants. It's her damn body."

"I know that. I'm not saying she couldn't do whatever she wanted."

"Don't start bullshitting me, Frank."

"I'm not."

"Yeah? Then what was that bullshit about getting an abortion if a baby got in the way?"

"It just came out wrong, that's all. Where're you going?"

"For a walk."

I was getting crucified for nothing. I wasn't for or against abortion. For Chrissake, when my ex-wife got pregnant while we were on the path to divorce, I was the one who suggested an abortion. It wouldn't have been good for the kid, and it certainly wasn't going to be the lifesaver she thought it was. I was grateful for the option and wouldn't deny a woman her choice.

Why did Mary Ann get so offended? Was I too obsessed with the case? Again? Was it her wanting to have a baby? I put my sneakers on and headed out the door to find her.

* * *

My head was pounding. I spilled out three aspirins and swallowed them with coffee. With a gross taste in my mouth, I looked through the overnight arrest activity. Thankful nothing had cropped up, I leaned back and closed my eyes.

"Out late last night?"

"Drank too much, Derrick."

"You? I'm surprised. Where'd you go?"

"Nowhere, me and Mary Ann had a fight. Over what? I couldn't tell you."

"Is everything okay?"

I yawned. "Yeah, nothing a couple of bottles of wine couldn't fix. How did you do with Norwicky's parents?"

"No problem. I picked up three water bottles and two cigarette butts."

My stomach turned over at the thought of a cigarette. "You sent them to the lab?"

"Yep. What's next?"

I forced myself to say, "I'm taking a ride to see Boyle's mother. You want to come along?"

"Definitely."

"Don't take this the wrong way, but this woman has been through more than anybody should have to. I'd like you to be in an observatory role. If you have something important, by all means, say it, but be tactful."

Chapter 45

Mrs. Boyle's thin smile crumpled into a frown when she saw Derrick. She took a tiny step back. "There's a break in the case?"

"Not yet, ma'am. This is my partner, Detective Dickson."

She shook his hand and said, "Please, come in."

There was that furniture polish smell again. We followed her to the same pair of couches. Sitting on the coffee table was another photo of young Debbie, this time in front of a school bus. It had to be her first day of school. Debbie had a pink backpack to go along with a ponytail and an ear-to-ear smile. I shoved aside the melancholy that was seeping in and said, "Thank you for seeing us again."

"That's okay. Finding Debbie's killer is the only thing that matters to me."

I wanted to ask, doesn't your son matter? "We appreciate your willingness to help, and you've been very helpful. I know it's difficult, but try to go on with your life. I'm going to stay on this until we bring whoever did this to justice."

Derrick's head bobbed.

"You don't understand; no one understands. You think catching whoever did this will make everything fine? Well, it won't!" She shook her head. "Don't get me wrong, I want the man who did this to my baby to pay, but it's not going to fix anything."

Man? Was that a general description for all males? "I understand, ma'am. All that I can do is what I promised, bring the perpetrator to justice."

"And for that I'd be thankful."

"I'm not certain if you knew about an incident that occurred at Barron High School. It was between your daughter and a student named Jason Norwicky."

Her dull eyes came to life. "He wouldn't leave Debbie alone. He'd keep calling, and Debbie would hang up on him. Finally, I had to tell him to stop calling."

"Do you know what the calls were about?"

"A misunderstanding of some sort. Debbie said he liked her, but she had no interest in him."

"When was the last time he called?"

The light in her eyes disappeared. "Just about a week before it happened."

"Did Debbie ever say that he threatened her?"

"Not threaten, just that he wouldn't leave her alone."

"I have a couple of questions that may upset you, but they're part of the investigation and it's information that I need. Okay?"

She put her hands in her lap and nodded.

"Why did Debbie quit cheerleading in the middle of a season?"

"She was bored with it. Debbie considered it childish, and frankly, I agreed with her. I was happy she was maturing."

"It wasn't injury related?"

"No, not at all."

"Was your daughter pregnant at the time of her death?"

Her cheek twitched. "Pregnant? I don't think so."

"When you were doing the laundry, did you notice any discharge on her underwear or bedsheets?"

I didn't know whose cheeks were redder, Mrs. Boyle's or Derrick's. Eyes fixed on her hands, she exhaled. "There was one time, I questioned her about it, and she said it was her period. I let it go, but honestly, she started doing the laundry herself. I was afraid she was having sex, and that's what it was. Do you know something I don't?"

"Like I said, we're exploring every possibility. Was your daughter sexually active?"

"I believe so. I told her several times to be careful."

"There was nothing in the file about her taking any birth control pills. Was she using anything?"

"Not that I am aware of. I should have known, but the OBGYN would never have told me if I asked, so I never did."

"There are privacy laws to protect patients. So, don't worry about it."

"Thanks."

"Would you mind if I took the ring we found in that turtle with us? We'd like to conduct a test on it. I'd return it as soon as possible."

"You want the ring?"

"If you wouldn't mind."

"That's okay with me. I didn't even know it was sitting there." She rose. "I'll get it."

"Thanks, and please don't touch the ring. Bring the turtle down. I'll remove the ring."

Her eyebrows shot up. "Oh. Okay." She disappeared down a hallway.

Derrick leaned in. "Man, she's washed out." He grabbed the school bus picture.

I whispered, "Put that down."

"She lives alone, right?"

"Yeah."

"The place smells like Lemon Pledge, and everything is so neat."

"You should see the kid's—" I shut my mouth when I heard her footsteps.

The victim's mother carried the turtle with both hands as if she were carrying eggs. She extended her arms, and I took the turtle. I set it down, removed its shell, and pulled on gloves.

I speared the ring with my pen, dropped it into a plastic evidence bag and handed it to Derrick, who recorded the date and place.

"Do you really think it was his ring? The person who did this?"

Derrick said, "We don't know, but the process of elimination is a critical component of the investigative process."

Well said, but he was watching too many crime shows on TV.

"Thank you again, Mrs. Boyle. We're done for today, but I'll be in touch."

The sound of the car door closing was still in the air when Derrick said, "How come we left so fast?"

"We got what we wanted, the ring, info on her being pregnant, and a little insight into Norwicky."

"He wouldn't leave Boyle alone. Badgering her and the mother."

"No doubt Norwicky was persistent. Let's see what the parents' DNA tells us."

"We should have it tomorrow."

"Good."

"You think the kid was pregnant?"

"Yep."

"I wish you wouldn't have told her to get the ring. I wanted to see the bedroom, like you did."

"Trust me, you don't need to see it. It's depressing."

"What are you going to do with the ring? Test it?"

"Might as well see if there's any DNA on it."

"More information. Right?"

I nodded.

"I kept quiet, like you said."

"Did you rehearse that line about the process of elimination in front of a mirror?"

Chapter 46

My shoulders sagged when I saw the IT guy sitting behind Derrick's desk.

"Good morning, Detective Luca."

"Morning, Marco. What's going on?"

"Just an update, sir."

"Am I going to lose anything again?"

"No, no. The last time had nothing to do with what we were doing."

"Yeah, just another coincidence."

He shrugged, and I powered up my computer. Halfway through my coffee, I was staring at a blinking cursor.

"Marco, tell me you didn't touch my computer."

"Why? What's the matter?"

"It's not turning on."

"Just wait, don't touch anything. It needs to cycle through the update."

Draining the last of my java, the screen flickered to life.

"It's back up."

There was an email from the Jacksonville school system. The subject line was Peter Morgan. I leaned toward the screen, clicked it open, and read.

Peter Morgan had moved to Jacksonville before the Boyle murder and was teaching there the day of the murder. He taught the entire day, and his last class ended at three thirty. Jacksonville was a solid seven hours away. I couldn't rule out the possibility, but unless Morgan was Clark Kent, it'd be impossible to pull off.

I could smell the coffee before Derrick came in with two cups. He rolled his eyes. "What's going on? Another update?"

"Yep. I think we can eliminate Morgan. He was in Jax teaching until three thirty."

"Last time I drove up there it took me almost ten hours."

I popped the top off the coffee—nice and dark. "Did you take the ring down to the lab?"

Derrick pulled his cell out. "Yeah, they've got it. They said the Norwicky parent report would be ready this afternoon. Uh, check out this email from Interpol."

The Interpol document was a compilation of reports from the Hellenic Police and the Russian version of the FBI, the Investigative Committee of Russia. Most of what was in the report were things we knew: that Papadakis was a suspect in the death of a boy in Greece, that the family had left Russia for Greece, and that Papadakis had ignored the requirement that he inform the Hellenic Police before traveling abroad.

What was new had been provided by the Russians. It was information regarding the assault of an Orthodox priest and the robbery of the daily collection. Boris Yenko, a sixty-eight-year-old who led the Cathedral of Christ the Savior, was nearly beaten to death immediately following a Mass.

The Papadakis family were members of the church, and Igor Papadakis was the only altar server at the morning Mass before the assault. Papadakis was questioned about the beating and burglary but not held. A day after the assault, the church realized that four valuable icons were missing.

Authorities believed that the icons were stolen after Father Yenko was incapacitated.

Papadakis was seen by a neighbor carrying a sack the morning after the attack on Father Yenko.

The police questioned Papadakis and searched the family home. Nothing was recovered, and the investigation petered out as the Soviet Union disintegrated. The icons remain missing today.

I said, "Can you believe this guy? He's trouble across continents."

"You think he beat up a priest?"

"No."

"Why? Because he was an altar server?"

"No. Because he's an opportunist."

"I don't get it."

"I think Papadakis witnessed the beating and robbery, using it as cover to steal the icons."

"What makes you think that?"

"As a server, he had no reason to beat the priest up to steal. I'm sure he had many opportunities and access if he wanted the money. I think he couldn't resist the chance the incident provided. Problem for him was that he was too stupid to realize he'd never be able to unload the icons."

"Hmmm."

"My hunch is the icons are sitting in that chest of his."

"Probably, but how do you think this impacts the Boyle case?"

"It's more evidence Papadakis is one depraved bastard with questionable judgment."

Chapter 47

Derrick said, "Without a match on Papadakis's DNA, we need something hard on him. Right now, all we have is smoke."

"From what I learned about serial killers, and I'm not saying he's one, people who kill between long spans of time are rare."

"Maybe we haven't caught enough of them, especially someone like Papadakis. This guy not only moved but moved across three continents; that's why there's no trace."

I didn't think so but said, "He may be smarter than we think."

"But we're onto him now."

"I'm not convinced."

I opened up Google translate and typed in Fred, looking for the Russian translation. Was it something like Igor? Up came Russian characters that bore no resemblance to English. I hit the speaker and it played back something sounding like Igor. Repeating the process, Igor in Greek sounded like Igor in English.

"Derrick, did Papadakis have a middle name?"

"Yeah, Misha. It's Russian for Michael. We should ask for a warrant."

Papadakis bothered me, but was he the Boyle killer? His DNA didn't match what was under the kid's nail, but I couldn't get that locked chest out of my mind. What was in there? The stolen icons? He'd be nuts to keep the murder weapon in there. I didn't want to ask for a search warrant. We didn't have enough, and I'd ruin my reputation going for something we had no legal right to. For a nanosecond I thought of asking Derrick to draft the request, but the kid didn't need to start off on the wrong foot.

"We don't have the basis for one. No judge would grant one."

"May not need it. The report on Norwicky's parents just came in.

I'll forward to it to you."

It didn't look like Norwicky was the killer. The DNA from under Boyle's nail did not match the mitochondrial DNA of Norwicky's mother.

"What does mitochondrial DNA mean?"

"It's a type of DNA we inherit from our mothers. Bottom line is, whoever left that DNA on the victim's nail, their mother wasn't Mrs. Norwicky."

"What if he was adopted? You know, had a different biological mother?"

I liked the way he was thinking. It was the way I did before chemo. "It's easy enough to check. Look up the birth records."

"I'm going to."

* * *

It was such a beautiful day that I was going to take Mary Ann for lunch at the Turtle Club. She was always asking to go, but since it was the place I'd met Kayla I shied away from taking her there.

I was glad to have called a buddy who tended bar there. A twenty-something in a low-cut blouse and tiny shorts took us through the restaurant and onto the deck. For a mid-January afternoon, the deck was busy.

Fate's hand directed us to the same table where I'd had lunch with Kayla.

"Is there something else available?"

"It's perfect, Frank. What's the matter?"

The girl said, "I'm sorry. If you'd like to wait at the bar until something opens up."

"Nah, it's okay."

"This table is wonderful, Frank."

I was tense and wanted a glass of wine to lubricate things. "You want a glass of wine?"

"Wine? We're working."

"One glass ain't going to impair you, Mary Ann."

Her eyes went cold. "It's against department rules, and you know it."

"Okay, okay. Just looking to celebrate our first time here."

She picked up the menu. "What do you usually get?"

"The basa fish sandwich. It's good."

"Basa? Where does that come from?"

"Somewhere in Asia."

"I'll stick to something from the Gulf."

We put in our order, and my phone pinged with a new email. Mary Ann and I had made a pact not to look at our phones when we were out. We couldn't believe all the people who sat at tables and played with their phones instead of interacting with each other. In fact, we instituted a rule when we were out to eat with friends: you put your phone in the middle of the table, and whoever picked theirs up had to pay the bill. It worked like magic.

My phone rang. A tingle ran across the base of my skull. I looked at Mary Ann. She nodded. It was the forensics lab. I answered, and the vibration increased.

"We have to go."

"What's going on?"

"The results on the Boyle ring came in, and you're not going to believe it, but they're a match."

Mary Ann stiffened. "Who is it?"

"The same guy whose DNA was under the victim's nail."

"But you don't know who that is."

I didn't need the reminder. "At the moment, no. But this is big. Let's go."

"Frank, the case is twenty-five years old. We're both hungry. It can wait a half an hour."

* * *

What did we have? Debbie Boyle knew her killer. She had to have had a romantic interest in him. Why else would she have his college ring? It was an older man, someone now around fifty-five. Maybe he had blond hair and probably went to Rutgers University or their graduate school.

I was leaning toward a teacher, but Papadakis was around the right age, had blond hair and a tarred history. Problem was his DNA didn't seem to match.

I revisited Debbie Boyle's senior yearbook and went straight to Fred Stark's class picture. Stark had sandy hair, though it was cut short. With a shit-eating grin and a boyish figure, he looked just a few years older than his students. There were fourteen females and only eight males in his class—a perfect mix for someone who might prey on impressionable girls.

Larry Culver had long, blond hair and a muscular build. If not for the red tie and white shirt, he could have passed as a surfer. I could see how a teenage girl could be drawn in by his good looks and relaxed vibe. The student sex mix was evenly split at eleven each.

I flipped to the events section. There was that Halloween picture of Culver with his arm around Boyle and another student. I studied his face. Was he drunk or high? It was hard to tell, but something seemed off.

A page dedicated to the theater group had a picture of two female students with their arms around a male teacher with graying hair. I didn't remember the kids in my high school showing such affection to the teachers. Most of the time we were bitching about the workload they gave us.

Barron High ran a number of programs to benefit the less fortunate. The picture of the Christmas party for the United Way caught my eye. Two pretty students were sitting on Santa's lap. He had his arms wrapped around their waists and was whispering in the ear of one of the girls. I couldn't tell what teacher it was, but it wasn't Stark or Culver.

There were many other pictures with both male and female teachers hugging and holding students' hands in ways that would get them in trouble today. I closed the yearbook. Inconclusive at best.

It was time to check the year of Culver's diploma and see what school Stark graduated from. Picking up the phone, I called Barron High School.

Chapter 48

"What in the hell are the odds of that?"

Derrick said, "What are you talking about, Frank?"

"Fred Stark and Larry Culver both graduated from Rutgers in 1984."

"They went to school together?"

"Damn it! I just said they graduated from Rutgers the same year."

"Okay, okay. That's the same year as the ring from Boyle's bedroom."

"Were these two bastards working together? It'd be hard to conceal a relationship with a student, but if each of them ran cover for the other, it'd get a lot easier."

"It makes me sick thinking of it. But you know, a lot of priests got away with stuff a hell of a lot worse."

"Parents trusted teachers back then. Today, if a teacher criticizes a kid the parents run and get a lawyer."

"It's crazy."

"It could be either of them or both of them."

"So, it's not Papadakis, then?"

"If you were listening, you'd know I was talking about a relationship, which may or may not have anything to do with her murder."

"But you think it did, right?"

"It makes a solid motive. Boyle could have threatened to reveal the relationship or could have been impregnated, which really would complicate things for a teacher."

"You sound like your leaning to it being Stark or Culver."

"We need DNA samples from them, then we'll know who the ring belongs to. Let them explain how their DNA got under her nails and what Boyle was doing with their ring."

"How could they explain that?"

"I don't know. Papadakis fits the profile, and it could be him, but either way, I'm going after these teachers. If they did what I think they did, they need to be held accountable. And if Boyle was pregnant and we could establish for how long, we might have a sex-with-a-minor felony case, though the statute of limitations passed."

"But Florida has special penalties if a teacher engages in it, don't we?"

"Yeah, but that's for them to handle upstairs. If we uncover this, Stark and Culver would be beyond disgraced; they'd be stripped of their pensions and run out of town."

"If I were a father, man, I'd kick some ass."

My desk phone rang. It was a meek-sounding friend of Joanne Wilbur's. As she talked, I waved at Derrick and gave him a thumbs-up. The call lasted a minute but opened a path forward.

"That was a woman who said she wanted to talk about Fred Stark."

Derrick shot out of his chair. "It's the break we needed. We gonna bring him in?"

"No. I'm going to see her. I want you to go see the DA, find out what we can or can't do with a twenty-five-year-old charge of sex with a minor. I don't even know if this woman was a minor at the time. Either way, let's get the legalities lined up."

* * *

Muriel Tulch lived in an old building on Vanderbilt Drive. Scaffolding encased the five-story structure, whose best feature was its Gulf view. The workers were listening to Spanish music and jackhammering the stucco. I climbed the outdoor stairs to the second floor and hit the bell twice.

The door cracked open and I announced myself. Tulch removed the chain and met my eyes briefly. I had to strain to hear her as she invited me in.

Muriel Tulch wasn't much to look at, but if she had a bust like this in high school, it explained the interest from a deviant like Stark. There was a family photograph in the foyer featuring two girls and a tall husband. It made me feel good that Tulch had survived whatever happened to her in high school. She was wearing a yellow sweater and black jeans.

Her place was small. The kids must be off to college. A great view of the Gulf offset the constrained feeling from the unit's low ceilings. Tulch circled around a glass kitchen table and pulled a chair out.

"Nice view."

"Normally, I'd have the sliders open, but with all the work being done . . ."

What? No offer of a drink or anything about the weather? "I want to thank you again for coming forward. It's brave of you."

"I put this behind me years ago, but when Joanne mentioned that you were checking into the teachers at Barron. I just . . . felt I had to say something."

"We're glad you did. Tell me about Fred Stark."

Tulch picked at a thumbnail. "Well, all the girls were captivated with him and Mr. C. They were handsome, independent, and they showed a lot of attention to us."

"What kind of attention?"

"Well, at first it was just routine encouragement. You know, saying nice things about how we looked, how smart we were, those kinds of things."

"Would you call it grooming?"

"I've thought about it, and in hindsight, I guess Mr. Stark, he did it without raising any alarms."

"What exactly did he do?"

"At first, when I was a junior, that's when he first touched me. Class was over, but I was having trouble with a project and stayed to show him. He was sitting at his desk, and I was standing next to him, leaning over. He—he put his arm around me and pulled me into him. He put his face right into my breast and wouldn't let go. I didn't know what to do. He said I—I felt nice, and then we went back to work."

"Things progressed from there?"

"I used to volunteer at the snack stand for the football games, and

I'd have to be there early, and he knew it. He started coming around, and one thing led to another, and we started to kiss and you know, touch each other."

I had to lean forward to hear her. "With your hands?"

She stared at the table and whispered, "Yes, he, I mean; I masturbated him."

"Was there any bodily penetration? Orally or otherwise?"

"No! Nothing that bad. It was just the masturbation."

"How old were you when this happened?"

"Seventeen."

"Did you know of any other teachers doing this?"

She blushed tomato red. "Mr. C started to get friendly, if you know what I mean. I'm sure Stark must have told him about us, that bastard."

"Did anything happen between you and Larry Culver?"

"No. But I'm pretty sure he was doing something, or trying to, anyway, with the girl who died."

"What makes you believe that?"

"I saw them arguing one time beneath the stands, before a game."

"Do you remember when that was?"

"It was a couple of days before she was killed."

Chapter 49

Stark tried brushing me off, telling me his wife was sick and he had to grade papers. He caved quickly when I said I'd interview him in the morning at the high school. Since he claimed his wife was ill, I suggested we meet down at Bayfront, a high-rise community with restaurants and a marina.

Stark was sitting at one of the outdoor tables at EJ's Café. He was wearing a Yankee baseball cap pulled down low. I dragged a metal chair out and sat. Stark had a wedding band but no Rutgers school ring.

Stark's hand trembled lifting his cup. "Would you like a coffee?"

"No."

Stark wiped cream off his lip. "I'm addicted to these Frappuccinos."

"Muriel Tulch."

I could smell the fear coming off him before her last name was out of my mouth.

"Excuse me?"

I leaned across the table. "Cut the bullshit, Mr. Stark. You know exactly who she is and what you did to her."

"I—I don't know what you're talking about. Honestly."

Nice. We got the invocation of honesty out of the way early. "I was hoping to have a frank discussion about what was going on at Barron High twenty-five years ago. Just so that you're aware, Muriel Tulch was very explicit in describing your relationship."

Stark hung his head. "I made a mistake, but that was a very long time ago. It was a one-time thing . . ."

"Spare me the regret. You crossed a big damn line, is what you did."

"Should I be getting a lawyer?"

"That's entirely up to you, but right now I just want to talk about Debbie Boyle."

"What about her?"

"Did you do anything with her or to her, like you did with Muriel Tulch?"

"No. I didn't. I swear."

He sweared. How comforting. "Do you know of anyone else who did?"

Stark paused too long. Either he did something or knew someone who did. "No, I don't know anything about that."

"Are you willing to submit a DNA sample?"

Starks eyes widened. "I don't think that's a good idea."

"I can do it here, discreetly; no one will know."

"No."

I wanted to spit on him. "Why are you still teaching? You must have enough time in to retire."

"I do, but I love teaching. I get a kick out of the kids."

There was no question he did. "Get out of here. I'm done with you."

"Really?"

I nodded, and he took off like a scared raccoon. I watched him until he was out of sight and took the coffee cup he had been drinking.

* * *

As I dipped a piece of twist bread in olive oil, Mary Ann said, "We're close to catching a cyber pervert. I'm going to be a decoy at the Golden Gate Starbucks."

"I don't like it. You can get hurt being bait."

"Don't worry, Frank. We have everything under control."

"You think you have it buttoned up, but you never know how he's going to react."

"It'll be fine."

"Who's running this? McGowan?"

"Yep."

"You tell him you want two men inside the store. Get one behind the counter and another posing as a customer."

"It's done already."

"Make sure there are at least two cars, engines running."

"We're going to have three."

"Don't forget—"

She put her hand on my arm. "Don't worry, Frank. I'm going to be fine. It's nothing to get concerned about."

"I don't want anything to go wrong."

"It won't."

"You know, if you, if you become a mother or something, you can't be doing this type of work."

She put her fork down and smiled. "If that day ever comes, I'll make sure I get assigned to desk duty. Okay?"

I nodded. "I'm not saying you'd get hurt or anything, but a kid, they don't know, they'd be worrying every time you left the house."

"What about you? They'd worry about their daddy too."

Daddy?

* * *

After a sleepless night imagining myself as a father, I was glad to be working on a Saturday. The idea of fatherhood became a mental tug-of-war. It'd be nice to have a child we could teach, but . . .

The thought of having a daughter was frightening. How could I protect her in a world like ours? There were creeps and perverts behind a lot of smiling faces. I'd arrested so many people who surprised their friends with their criminality that I stopped counting.

Look at the dirtbags in the Boyle case. Stark and Culver preyed on young girls, and Papadakis, who knew what he was capable of? Even the guys we cleared were no winners. If my daughter ever brought someone like them home, I'd stroke out.

There were a lot of bad men out there. Men who wanted nothing but sex. Men who wanted to dominate their wives. Who'd suppress their dreams, kill their spark.

The chances of getting a good guy were slim, and that's if the kid was born without any medical issues. That was another risk, and adding to it, Mary Ann wasn't as young as most mothers. I knew women were having kids later, but there was a lot of research that reinforced the risks older mothers faced.

The world was too dangerous, and in combination with Mary Ann's age, my mind was leaning against the idea of fatherhood as I turned onto Crayton Court.

Larry Culver lived in a whitewashed ranch that was built in the sixties. His home was dwarfed by two new homes: a brown behemoth built in a Mediterranean style, and a sleek coastal contemporary home, painted a light gray.

Forcing a ring on to my finger, I noticed a father trailing behind a boy on a bike with training wheels. The father smiled like his kid had scaled Mount Everest. The kid circled and stopped in front of their driveway.

"Daddy! Daddy, I did it!"

The father scooped his son off the bike. "I know. See, you can do anything!"

I felt my cheeks spreading into a smile and clapped. "Way to go, way to go!"

The kid waved at me, wriggled free and got back on his bike. He looked like Bert. I gave a thumbs-up to the father and walked to the door of Culver's home.

A black cat was curled up on an Adirondack chair, soaking up the sun. It opened one green eye before resuming its nap.

The bell chime was still resonating when the door opened. Culver had been watching for me. He was wearing a long-sleeved, white shirt and beige chinos. On a Saturday morning? Though there was a hint of bags beneath them, his hazel eyes still sparkled.

"Good morning, Detective. Come on in."

"Morning." I stepped into a house that had new wooden floors.

A woman in exercise clothes stepped into the hallway holding a cup of coffee. "Good morning, would you like a cup of coffee?"

"Sure, thanks."

The kitchen had cabinets that had been repainted an off-white and were capped by a veiny, beige marble. As his wife poured my cup, another cat, this one a tabby, jumped onto the counter.

"Get off of there, Fred."

"Fred?"

"Larry likes to name his cats Fred."

Did he also write messages under their names?

"Not all of them. I've only had three."

"No, it's been at least four."

"All right already. We're going to sit out on the lanai."

I was surprised by the large, crescent-shaped lake. No wonder his neighbors had sunk so much money into their homes.

"This is nice. You have long views in both directions."

"It's a great setting. We've been here almost twenty years, but it's changed." He pointed to his Mediterranean neighbor.

I took a sip of coffee. "Like they say, there's a plus and a minus to everything."

He nodded and picked up an electronic cigarette that was on the glass table.

"I came down here from Jersey, so I can't complain about anything. Say, that reminds me, I saw your diploma in your office. You went to Rutgers, so you know all about New Jersey, don't you?"

He blew a cloud of smoke out of the side of his mouth. "I guess so."

I couldn't detect a smell from the smoke. "Rutgers is a good school. Even their football team is up there these days."

"It was a good fit. Had some of my best years there. Even met my wife there."

"You must have a lot of that school spirit, then."

"I was active, for sure."

"I went to John Jay." I pointed to my school ring. "Where's your ring?"

He shrugged. "It's been a long time. I don't know where it could be."

"Really?"

"Do you work on Saturday mornings to investigate missing rings?"

"Would you rather we speak at your school?"

He frowned and took a sip of coffee.

"You've been a teacher, and now the principal of Barron High, for over thirty years. I asked you about it the last time we met, and I'll ask again. Were members of the faculty engaged in inappropriate relationships with students?"

"That's a serious accusation to infer, Detective."

"I'm not inferring. I'm asking a direct question and expect an honest answer."

The vein in his temple started to beat. "I've been principal for almost ten years now and have no knowledge of any such behavior."

"And how about the twenty years before that?"

"I wasn't in a leadership capacity at that time. My role was purely as a teacher."

"Your colleague, Mr. Stark, was a teacher, yet he, shall we say, was more than knowledgeable."

"Are you going to ask me for a DNA sample as well?"

Stark and Culver had talked. Did they have a plan? "Would you like to voluntarily submit one?"

He took a long drag on his device. "Your interest in things that may have happened long ago is surprising."

"Why do you find that puzzling?"

"The statutes of limitations would have expired years ago for whatever transgressions you seem to think happened."

He was a smartass. But knowing the law was an admission he'd abused his position as a teacher. What other reason was there to know the statutes?

"That's true, but there is no statute of limitation for murder."

He didn't flinch. "Do you really believe Fred Stark murdered Debbie Boyle?"

Was Culver shifting the attention to Stark? "If you are aware of a connection and refuse to divulge it, you'd be obstructing justice at the least and possibly be an accessory to murder."

Culver set the e-cigarette on the table. "Fred Stark and I have worked together for thirty-odd years. He's a good man and a good teacher, but like the rest of us, he's not perfect."

"Not perfect? A bad dresser? Curses too much? Or is he a sexual predator?"

"Predator? That's not the man I know."

My pee-pee alarm beeped. "I'm sorry, I've got to run, or I'll be late for my next appointment."

Culver rose as soon as I said the word run. "Oh, you'd better go, then."

He slid the sliders open and stepped back into the house. I followed him for a couple of steps before turning around, "Oh, I forgot my phone." I hurried outside, picked up the e-cigarette and swapped places with my phone.

"I got it."

Culver swung the door open, and the black cat darted through his legs into the house. Was that bad luck? For who?

Chapter 50

As soon as I got in the car, I sent a text to Derrick. We needed a sample of Culver's handwriting, and it hit me that yearbooks always had a letter signed by the principal. Were the new memory supplements Mary Ann bought working?

Culver would realize I took his device before I got to Pine Ridge. I didn't care—information was information. If my hunch was right, I'd worry later about getting evidence that would hold up in court. I bagged the e-cigarette and pulled away. It was ten forty-five. I could drop the evidence at the forensic lab and make the BBQ at our neighbor's house by two.

Every Saturday the forensic lab was sanitized. Stepping into their foyer, the bleach smell burned my nose. The reception desk was empty. I signed in and rang the bell. I was about to hit the buzzer again when I saw Miller, a senior tech, through the door's narrow window.

The lower buttons of his lab coat were open. Hurrying to the door, the bottom of his coat looked like a mermaid's tail. A frown formed on his face when he saw me through the window. The locks whirled, and the door swung open.

"Detective Luca. What is it that brings you here on a Saturday?"

I held up the bag. "I need a DNA profile on this ASAP. Then, we'll need it cross-referenced against the DNA from the Boyle case."

The frown returned. "The twenty-five-year-old Boyle case?"

"Yes, Debbie Boyle, an innocent seventeen-year-old who was brutally stabbed to death at Delnor-Wiggins Park."

He checked his watch. "I don't know if I'll have the time. There are only two of us working today."

"I'm sorry, I hate to ask, but we're on the cusp of a breakthrough in the case."

He shook his head. "That's exactly what your partner said when he wanted—no, it was demanded—an analysis of a handwriting sample."

"Oh, I didn't realize that. Were you able to do the handwriting analysis?"

"No. Ryan isn't working today."

"Damn. I was hoping I wouldn't have to wait till Monday."

He smiled. "It's going to be longer than that; he's off until Wednesday."

"Wednesday? Are you kidding me?"

"Patience, Detective. After all, it's an old case; what's the hurry?"

I wanted to ask him if he'd like to tell that to Boyle's mother. "Did he go away?"

"No. A couple of his friends are in town."

"Okay, but I'll need the DNA profile on the e-cigarette."

He nodded slightly and turned on his heels.

* * *

It was just after noon. Ryan was a golfer. I hoped like hell his guests liked early tee times. It would take me twenty minutes to get to his house in Naples Lakes. I was about to call Mary Ann but opted on sending a text. I pulled out of the parking lot and drove to see Ryan.

The sound of my crest falling probably reached Maine. Ryan had taken his friend to La Playa for a round of golf. Why would he pay for a round of golf? Naples Lake was a bundled community, meaning everyone had to pay for golf, whether you used it or not.

It was a struggle to be polite to his wife. One of their houseguests happened to be from New Jersey and wanted to discuss the taxes it sucked out of its residents. The pull to flee Jersey was almost as powerful as the feeling I had now. Invoking urgent police business, I said goodbye.

The traffic had thickened, and it was half past one when I turned onto Immokalee. I made a left, crossing the bridge where we'd found one of the serial killer's victims floating in a drainage canal. I sped toward the golf club.

La Playa had a popular hotel and beach club on Vanderbilt Drive, but not being a golfer, I'd never been to their golf course. I navigated to a building where an army of golf carts were parked. I scanned for Ryan, but with everyone wearing colored golf shirts and shorts, you'd have to be Andre the Giant to stand out.

There was a large outdoor patio filled with golfers looking for refreshments. I snaked through, but Ryan was nowhere to be found. It was time to elevate things.

Flashing my badge to the concierge brought a look of concern and privacy. Explaining that an important police matter necessitated the need to locate Ryan, the concierge summoned a caddy, who headed for the higher-numbered holes.

A call from Mary Ann came in. It was a couple of minutes before two. Swiping the call away, I sent a text saying that I'd meet her at our neighbor's house. She didn't respond.

Ryan swiped the baseball cap off his head, grimacing when he saw me. He hopped off the cart, said something to his friend, and pointed to the bar.

"It better be good, Luca."

"I'm sorry, buddy, but I need you to take a look at something for me on the Boyle case."

"You pulled me off the course for the Boyle case?" He pointed to the bar, where his friend had gone. "See that guy over there? He was my best man, and I haven't seen him in almost ten years."

"I'm sorry, really. This won't take long. They told me you wouldn't be back until Wednesday, and there's no way I could last that long."

"Well, you're going to have to."

"It's just one sample. I don't need anything formal, just your opinion on whether it matches with who wrote the yearbook message."

His eyes bore into me. "Okay, but just something informal."

"Thanks."

He looked at his watch. "We're on the seventeenth hole. I'll be done in twenty minutes. Meet me at the lab in forty-five."

Mary Ann was going to be pissed, but I couldn't wait until Wednesday. It was easier sending a text that I was going to be late. Within a second of hitting send she responded, "How could you? BILLY is waiting for you!" I had told the kid I was going to play catch with him, teaching him to catch pop-ups.

It was four thirty-five when I opened the screen door to our neighbor's covered lanai. Everyone was seated around a table filled with fruit and desserts. Billy was chewing on a brownie. He smiled when he saw me and started to get up. Mary Ann shook her head, told him to stay, and met me.

She whispered, "Where were you? Billy's been looking for you all afternoon."

"We got a break on the Boyle case. The handwriting in the yearbook is probably Culver's."

"Probably? You disappointed Billy over a probably?"

"No, it's . . . not like that."

"Then what's it like?"

A text notification sounded as Billy came running over with his glove and ball. Mary Ann said, "I shouldn't have, but I made you a plate. It's in the kitchen."

"Hey, Billy! Sorry, pal. Something urgent came up in a case I'm working." I dug out my phone. The text was from the forensics lab.

Chapter 51

Sundays always passed quickly, but not yesterday. I was pissed at Miller. His text said he hadn't had time to run the DNA tests on Culver's electronic cigarette. Did I make a mistake in pushing him?

I'd left two messages with the lab before heading to the shooting range. If I put off my recertification requirements any longer I'd lose my firearm privileges. We had a nice range in the basement of the building, next to the room that held the ballistics tank.

Signing in, I was given two boxes of ammo, earmuffs, and targets. I put my ear protection on and was buzzed into the chamber. A single officer was popping off rounds in the middle booth. My pistol proficiency had always been good, but for some reason I was only an okay shot with a rifle.

Holding my breath, I squeezed off my first shot—bull's-eye. Seven of my first eight shots were dead center. I reloaded and shot rapidly. It felt good to concentrate on shooting. I swapped out targets, putting up a human silhouette. I aimed for and hit both knees. Then I moved to each of the shoulders. Two for two again.

The gunsmith commented over the loudspeaker on my shooting, and I gave him a thumbs-up. Reeling in the target, I knew I had it today and wished I'd brought a rifle with me. The day was off to a good start. The question running through my mind as I climbed the stairs was whether it would continue.

* * *

As I sat, Derrick said, "How'd you do?"

"Nothing but bull's-eyes."

"Really?"

"Yep." My cell buzzed. I dug it out. It was Miller from the lab. I stood and answered. Listening, I pumped my fist.

Derrick jumped out of his chair when I told him and said, "Let's arrest his ass!"

"Hold on."

"Hold on? We got him."

"We're going to need to get as much as possible out of him. I talked to the DA yesterday, and he's very concerned about getting a conviction, even with the nail DNA match."

"Why?"

"A, it's twenty-five-year-old evidence that wasn't cataloged. The defense will claim it's been planted. B, we can't place him at the scene, and C, the motivation is circumstantial. He gave it less than a fifty-fifty chance we get a conviction and said unless we get more, not to arrest him."

Dickson said, "But we know he preyed on her."

I nodded. "I know. End of the day, the more we have, the easier it will be to get a conviction. We arrest him now, and he'll hire a lawyer."

"What are we going to do?"

"I want to talk to him before he gets a mouthpiece. See if he gives us anything."

"Man, I can't wait. We're going to do it here, right?"

"No. He'd lawyer up if we pulled him in. I'm trying to decide if I should do it at his house or at the school."

"I say the school. We go there; he'll be crapping in his pants."

"We need him as relaxed as possible. We'll do it at his house. We'll have a better shot of getting something out of him."

* * *

The sun was shining, but there was a chill in the air. It was the first week of February and not unusual to be cool, especially in the morning. Derrick rang the bell, and I turned around to face the sun.

Culver opened the door. The only thing crisp about him was his shirt. It was obvious he didn't get much sleep last night. He looked at us and then at his watch. Culver wanted us to come after his wife went to a yoga class. I agreed, but wanting his wife to add pressure, I went back on my word.

"Come on in." We followed him into the kitchen. "Would you like some coffee?"

We said no in stereo as his wife came in holding a rolled-up mat. "Is everything all right, Larry?"

"Yes, just some school business, that's all."

"Okay, I'll see you later."

Culver pecked his wife's cheek and said to us, "Let's sit here; the sun hasn't warmed things up yet."

I said, "Give it an hour. It'll be in the seventies."

Culver pulled a red e-cigarette out. "What did you want to see me about? Mr. Stark?"

"No. You inferred that Peter Morgan was a teacher who may have had a relationship with a student. Was that a head fake?"

He took a long pull, turned his head, and blew out the smoke. "Not at all. You asked me about who could have done such a thing, and he came to mind. He was popular with the girls."

"Well, that's funny, because he said you and Larry Stark were the popular ones."

"Really? He said that?"

"He also said he believed you were having a relationship with Debbie Boyle."

Culver twirled the smoking device with his fingers. "What would give him that impression?"

"Morgan said he saw the two of you alone in a classroom, and Boyle was crying."

"Oh yeah, I remember that. She was upset about her father being gone. It might have been his birthday."

"Muriel Tulch also saw the two of you under the stands before a football game."

He took a drag. "I have no recollection of that."

"Do you recall writing a message in Boyle's yearbook?"

"Absolutely not."

"Are you sure about that? Our handwriting expert said the message left under the name of Fred matches yours."

"Can't be."

"Telephone records document nine calls between your house and the Boyle home. What did you call her about?"

"I don't remember calling her, but if I did, it was regarding schoolwork."

"But she wasn't in your class at that time."

"She would ask me for help from time to time."

"Were you having an affair with Debbie Boyle?"

"No."

"How do you explain the fact that Debbie Boyle had your Rutgers school ring?"

"She did? How? I don't understand how you can say it was my ring. Rutgers has thousands of students. Even Frank went to Rutgers. It's probably his."

"It has your DNA on it."

"That doesn't prove anything. She probably stole it off my desk. My fingers swell, and I used to take it off from time to time."

"How do you explain your DNA being under Debbie Boyle's fingernail when she was murdered?"

His face went blank, but he recovered quickly. "I have no idea. Maybe you planted it, just like you stole my vapor. You cost me forty bucks, by the way."

"You're not going to need money where you're going."

"Is that a threat, Detective? I'll tell my lawyer you stole from me and are threatening me."

"I welcome talking to your lawyer."

"Look, this is an ancient case, and none of these allegations will stick in a court of law."

"Maybe not, but I'll guarantee you that once the school learns about all of this you'll be finished."

"The school will stand behind me. I will fight these allegations. There's no proof."

"We'll show them the love letter we found in Debbie's room that she wrote to you."

Culver squinted and stood. "It's time to leave, gentlemen."

Chapter 52

"I still can't believe you pulled that love letter thing on him. When you said it, I thought you'd been holding something back."

"I'd never do that."

"Culver looked like he was gonna die right there."

"He held it together better than I expected, but it had the desired effect. He's definitely going nuts now."

"I loved it, but"—he leaned in— "can we really do that type of stuff—lie to a suspect?"

"Why not? They lie to us all the time."

"True, but are the courts okay with it?"

"You can make a statement, and they can refute it. Plain and simple."

"Makes sense."

"Damn right. It was something he never expected, and he'll be staying up trying to figure out what she may have written."

"Not knowing is the worst. It makes you crazy."

"We need a way to add more pressure on Culver. If we do, he may cave."

"What are you thinking?"

"The way I think it went down is that he impregnated her, and she either was going to keep the baby or go public about their relationship. That would have destroyed Culver; he'd go to jail for sex with a minor. So, he confronts her. He threatens her. Their fight spins out of control and he stabs her to death. He went with a knife. It may not have been completely premeditated, but there's no doubt he had malice aforethought."

"Exactly, Frank. You thinking of offering a deal for manslaughter?"

"I'd like to, just to see how he reacts, but it's not my decision. Culver needs to know that we are serious about charging him. I'll check upstairs, but it might be time to bring him in."

"When're you thinking?"

"Tomorrow. I'm going to see the DA, then I'll call Culver."

* * *

I called the school twice, but they told me Culver was busy. The third time, I told the receptionist that if he didn't get on the phone, I was coming to talk to him in person. Sure enough, Culver got on the line.

"Detective Luca, I'm very busy. We're in the middle of midterms this week."

"This won't take long, Mr. Culver. You're going to have to come in tomorrow morning. Nine o'clock sharp."

"Come in?"

"Yes, the sheriff's office."

"But why? We talked earlier."

"The DA wants to talk to you."

"About what?"

"Not sure exactly, but maybe to offer you a plea, you know, from first-degree murder to manslaughter."

"Oh my God, no."

"I'm really not certain, but I'd recommend getting an attorney. If you can't afford one I believe the county will provide one for you."

* * *

The next day was going to be interesting. The DA's concerns about the age of the evidence and the circumstances surrounding the discovery of the nail fragment were overridden by Sheriff Chester's support of bringing him in.

As the day came to an end, I was surprised that I hadn't heard that Culver had retained a lawyer. It made me suspicious, and I was expecting to get sandbagged in the morning with a refusal to appear.

As annoying as it would be to receive a request to delay an

appearance, I forced myself to be okay with it. If Mrs. Boyle could wait twenty-five years, I could wait another couple of days.

My hand on the light switch, the phone rang. I grabbed the receiver and listened. Everything had just changed.

Chapter 53

A small crowd of people circled a woman in the driveway who was sobbing uncontrollably. Two uniformed officers were stationed by the front door. I signed in and pulled on gloves and booties.

"Where's the body?"

"The garage. It's on the left."

I stepped into the house and closed the door as the woman let out a wail. The first door was the laundry room. I paused a moment, steeled myself, and opened the garage door. Stepping in, a wave of heat and nausea hit me.

A rope hung down from the attic access. It was tied around the neck of a man whose back faced me.

An image of Barrow, the innocent kid who'd hung himself his first night in a cell, flooded my mind. My first case was haunting me again. I pushed the kid out of my mind and circled the body.

The drop wasn't long enough to break his neck. Larry Culver had died an excruciating death by strangulation. I swallowed hard and took a step closer.

Culver, in shorts and a blue golf shirt, swayed ever so slightly. There was no doubt he was dead. I felt his leg—cool, but no sign of rigor mortis. He was dead a couple of hours, not more. How long after I'd called? A tinge of guilt skimmed in and out of my head. Culver was responsible for his death, not me.

It was difficult to look at his face. I circled the body. A piece of paper was peeking out of his rear pocket. Suicide note? I grabbed a ladder he'd used and propped it by Culver. Pulling the paper out brought Culver's body within an inch of my face. Was a homicide detective supposed to get the heebie-jeebies?

I unfolded the note. It was addressed to his wife and daughter. I had forgotten about his daughter. This was a nasty business I was in.

> My Dearest Marilyn and Emily,
>
> I hope you can find it in your hearts to forgive me.
>
> Leaving both of you is the hardest thing I have ever done.
>
> Regrettably, it is impossible for me to continue knowing the hurt I have caused you and the shame I have cast on myself and my beloved school.
>
> Though it is difficult to understand, my decision to depart from this world is best for all of us.
>
> I am not attempting to minimize my actions, but you should know it was accidental and that the indiscretion with Debbie Boyle was singular in nature.
>
> With all my love, Lawrence

I read it twice. Was he a coward, or had he taken the brave way out? Either way, he did me a favor with his desire to avoid disgrace. A seasoned defense attorney would have had a good chance of getting him off the hook at a trial.

We needed to check for foul play, but this looked like suicide. I took a picture of Culver's note and bagged the original. Mrs. Culver had a right to see the note, but it was a delicate matter. Culver's family was innocent, and nothing was to be gained by publicizing the reason Larry Culver took his life.

I'd leave it to the sheriff to decide about releasing information. I would question Mrs. Culver and share the note with her. Like I said, this was a nasty business I was in. The coroner wasn't due for a while, so I hopped in the Jeep.

∗ ∗ ∗

Mrs. Boyle's smile quickly vanished. Her eyes searched my face as I stood in the doorway. She knew, and I nodded in acknowledgment.

She stepped aside, softly saying, "Please, come in."

We made a beeline to her couches. Me, looking at a picture of Debbie on a roller coaster, she asking, "Who did it?"

"We believe it was Larry Culver, a teacher and now principal at Barron High."

"Are you sure?"

"Yes, we have evidence. Though some of it is circumstantial, I'm confident it was him."

"That bastard. I'll kill him myself—"

"There's no need for that; he committed suicide."

"What?"

"He hung himself in his garage a couple of hours ago."

"So, he's a goddamn coward too?"

I shrugged. "He left a note referencing your daughter, but it wasn't an outright confession. What we believe happened is that Culver and your daughter had a romantic relationship that included sexual relations."

Her shoulder's sagged. "How could he?"

"It's disgusting, and he wasn't the only one."

"You mean my Debbie had another, uh, relationship with a different teacher?"

"No, no. What I meant was that we uncovered other instances of impropriety involving other students and teachers. It was not limited to your daughter."

She shook her head. "Unbelievable, really. How the hell could this have been going on?"

I had no answer, but boy, was I glad I wasn't around back then. "I'm sorry."

"Why was my daughter the only one who ended up murdered?"

"We believe she was either going to reveal their relationship or was impregnated by Culver and wanted to keep the baby."

Her head dropped, and she began sobbing. I got her a box of tissues and tried to console her. I wished Mary Ann was here and that I didn't have to talk with Mrs. Culver after this.

* * *

It was an awfully emotional day—two families shattered in just a few hours. It was late, and I was exhausted, but this was my last visit before going home. I jabbed the doorbell and it swung open. Fred Stark's eyes widened.

I said, "Step outside."

He hesitated before taking a single step forward. I took his wrist and pulled him onto the walkway. Stark looked like he was about to puke. I put my nose an inch away from his.

"In the morning, you're going to walk into Barron High and hand your papers in. You're leaving tomorrow. You want your pension, you do as I say. You hear me?"

Stark nodded.

"You stay past lunch, I swear I'll get your story in the papers and you'll get nothing. Anyone asks why the sudden change of heart, you tell them it's because of Culver's suicide. Now, what are you doing tomorrow?"

"But what, what'll I tell my wife?"

"I don't give a damn what you tell her. Just make sure you do as I say, or you'll regret it like nothing else in your life."

Chapter 54

It was a week since Culver had hung himself. I should have felt good with a solve on a cold case, but I didn't. Chester had acted like a peacock, and it pissed me off. The only thing good was taking advantage of Chester to get him to press for a search of Papadakis's garage.

I was disgusted that the focus was on the sexual scandal and not on the murder of Debbie Boyle. Did we really need further proof that sex sells?

The media had moved on to an outbreak of Legionnaires' disease at the Immokalee casino, but changes were afoot in the county school district. After a tumultuous public hearing, new rules governing the interaction between students and teachers were hashed out, and an authorization to fund the installation of cameras throughout each school was passed.

I was wondering if it was enough when my phone rang.

"Mrs. Boyle, how are you?"

"I'm actually doing much better, Detective Luca."

"That's good to hear."

"I just wanted to thank you for all that you've done for Debbie. Without you, we'd never have known what happened to her."

"Thank you, ma'am. It's my job, and the least we can do for you."

"Well, Brian and I appreciate it; we really do."

"I'm glad we were able to figure this out, but wish so many years hadn't passed."

"I know I told you it wouldn't change things, but I have to tell you that it did. I feel like I can try to move on now. In fact, I'm thinking of moving into something smaller, something closer to the water."

"That sounds great. A new home, a fresh start. I'm sure it'll all work out for you."

* * *

Two suitcases were open on the floor of our bedroom. Two pieces of luggage for four days? I didn't even want to go to Key West. I don't fish, and we have great beaches right here. The only thing that kept me from losing it was the pink negligee at the top of a pile of clothes.

"What are you doing, Mary Ann?"

"Packing. I didn't hear you come in."

"You think you have enough clothes?"

"I'm not taking both, Frank. The zipper is broken on the brown one."

"Oh." Holding your tongue did have merit from time to time. "Mrs. Boyle called me right before I left."

"What did she say?"

"She wanted to thank me. She said she was going to try to move on with her life, maybe even move out of that house."

"I don't understand how anyone could live in the same place. It's a constant reminder."

"I know. It's good to see her trying."

"Oh, did you see the picture on the counter?"

"No, what picture?"

"The one Bert made for you. I had it framed. It looks so cute. You really made an impression on him."

Uh-oh. Is this her lead-in to get talking about having a child? Can't I have a couple of days off before I have to start making life-changing decisions?

"Thanks. I'll bring it to the office when we get back."

"What time you want to leave tomorrow?"

"I don't know, maybe eight? We'll get there around two."

"Sounds good. I'm going to get dinner started."

"Okay."

As Mary Ann brushed past me, my cell rang. I pulled it out. "Uh-oh."

"What's the matter?"

"It's Chester."

Hands on hips, she said, "We're going away. I don't care what's going on."

"Hello, Sheriff."

"Hi, Frank. Something has come up."

"What's that, sir?"

"You were right on Papadakis. The chest had the missing icons in them."

THE END

Dan has a monthly newsletter that features his writing, articles on Self Esteem & Confidence building, as well as educational pieces on wine.

He also spotlights other author's books that are on sale. Sign up -

www.danpetrosini.com

Other Books by Dan Petrosini

Third Chances – A Luca Mystery Book 4

The Serenity Murder – A Luca Mystery Book 3

Vanished – A Luca Mystery Book 2

Am I the Killer? – A Luca Mystery Book 1

The Final Enemy

Complicit Witness

Push Back

Ambition Cliff

Coming Soon – Book 6 - A Luca Mystery

Thank you for taking the time to read A Cold, Hard Case. If you enjoyed it, please consider telling a friend or posting a short review where you obtained the book. Word of mouth is an author's best friend and is appreciated. Thank you, Dan

Printed in Poland
by Amazon Fulfillment
Poland Sp. z o.o., Wrocław